DISNEY · SQUARE ENIX

KINGDOM HEARTS Re:coded

THE NOVEL

Tomoco Kanemaki

Original Concept
Tetsuya Nomura
Daisuke Watanabe

Illustrations
Shiro Amano

YEN ON

NEW YORK

KINGDOM HEARTS RE:CODED
TOMOCO KANEMAKI,
ILLUSTRATIONS: SHIRO AMANO,
ORIGINAL CONCEPT: TETSUYA NOMURA, DAISUKE WATANABE

Translation by Luke Baker
Cover art by Shiro Amano

Yen On
150 West 30th Street, 19th Floor
New York, NY 10001

Visit us at yenpress.com
facebook.com/yenpress
twitter.com/yenpress
yenpress.tumblr.com
instagram.com/yenpress

First Yen On Edition: August 2019

Yen On is an imprint of Yen Press, LLC.
The Yen On name and logo are trademarks of Yen Press, LLC.

The publisher is not responsible for websites (or their content) that are not owned by the publisher.

Library of Congress Cataloging-in-Publication Data
Names: Kanemaki, Tomoko, 1975- author. | Amano, Shiro, illustrator. | Baker, Luke, translator.
Title: Kingdom hearts re:coded / Tomoco Kanemaki ; illustration by Shiro Amano ; translation by Luke Baker.
Description: First Yen On edition. | New York, NY : Yen On, 2019. | "Original concept: Tetsuya Nomura, Daisuke Watanabe"
Identifiers: LCCN 2019019407 | ISBN 9781975385392 (pbk.)
Subjects: | CYAC: Fantasy. | Adventure and adventurers—Fiction.
Classification: LCC PZ7.1.K256 Kg 2019 | DDC [Fic]—dc23
LC record available at https://lccn.loc.gov/2019019407

ISBNs: 978-1-9753-8539-2 (paperback)
978-1-9753-5873-0 (ebook)

1 3 5 7 9 10 8 6 4 2

LSC-C

Printed in the United States of America

CONTENTS

GOOD-BYE.

This is all I can do to atone for lying all this time. If we never see each other again, if you forget me—that's how it has to be. After all, everything happened because I wasn't brave enough.

But then you said something.

No, not good-bye!

I didn't understand what you meant, and I shook my head quietly.

When I wake up, I'll find you. And then there will be no lies. We're gonna be friends for real. Promise me, Naminé.

A promise...

You're going to forget making that promise, though. You won't remember me at all when you wake up.

I wanted to believe you. And I feel like I can have faith you will remember me. After all, it's you, Sora.

You have so many memories built up inside you. If the chain of memories comes apart, the links will still be there. The memory of our promise will always be inside you somewhere.

That is what I choose to believe.

CHAPTER 1
Disney Castle

JIMINY CRICKET GAZED AT HIS PAIR OF JOURNALS AND reflected on his two long adventures in one of the many rooms of Disney Castle, the world under King Mickey's rule. The king, Donald Duck, and Goofy were resting after their journeys, spending their time with Queen Minnie, Daisy Duck, and Pluto.

Jiminy had accompanied them in these quests to save the world twice—once to stop the darkness from spreading, and the other to put all the lost hearts where they belonged. Though both journeys had been difficult, Jiminy hadn't actually done any of the fighting. His role was as a recordkeeper.

After all was said and done, these records of their travels were all he had to show for his efforts. As he flipped through the volumes, Jiminy thought about the boy and his friends who had done the real adventuring.

But the pages of the first journal were all still blank—except for a single line:

Thank Naminé.

Well, maybe it was because those were the only words the book was meant to hold.

As Jiminy flipped through the blank pages, his heart stirred with emotion. He could vividly see in his mind's eye everything that had happened to Sora, Donald, and Goofy. It brought a smile to his face.

That was when it happened. Jiminy's breath caught in his throat as he discovered more text on one page of his supposedly blank journal:

Their hurting will be mended when you return to end it.

He had never seen this passage before—yet he had no memory of writing it.

Jiminy snapped the journal shut and rushed out of the room, hurrying down the corridor to the study of the king—Mickey.

"Your Majesty! Your Majesty!"

Jiminy burst through the small door nested in the corner of the larger one, too worked up to even knock, and sprang onto the desk of a slightly perplexed Mickey.

"Whoa, what's the matter, Jiminy?"

"It's the journal! There's a message I've never seen before!" He held the tiny book out before Mickey.

"A mysterious message?"

"Uh-huh. I certainly didn't write it. And you know I never once let the journal out of my sight."

Mickey peered closely at Jiminy's journal. Since Jiminy was a great deal smaller than him, the journal was positively miniscule.

"I don't know when anybody woulda had a chance to..."

Jiminy tilted his head to one side, while Mickey folded his arms.

"'Their hurting will be mended'? Gosh, Jiminy. Sounds like somebody needs help and doesn't know what to do. Let's get to the bottom of this."

"Of course, but how?" Jiminy asked uneasily as he looked up at Mickey. "All the other pages are completely blank."

"Sure, the words you wrote are gone, but that doesn't mean the journal is empty."

Mickey nodded with a smile and stood.

A few hours later, two small figures were busily scurrying about in the king's study—the chipmunk brothers, Chip and Dale. The pair were setting up some sort of large machine, with an enormous monitor and keyboard attached to it.

Donald and Goofy watched them curiously.

"Do you know what they're up to?" Donald asked.

"Nope." Goofy shrugged, equally baffled.

"They're gonna extract the memories from my journal."

"Huh?" Donald tilted his head at Jiminy's explanation.

"You see, the journal should still contain the memories of the worlds I wrote about when we visited."

"But wasn't it all erased?" Also confused, Goofy tilted his head even farther to the side than Donald had.

"Well, sure, the *words* disappeared, but the memories should still be there, at least according to my theory. If we convert the journal to data and analyze it, maybe we can find some clues," Mickey explained earnestly as he watched Chip and Dale hard at work.

The explanation did nothing to help Donald and Goofy.

"Your Majesty! Everything's ready!"

"Your Majesty! What Chipper said!" Chip and then Dale shouted toward Mickey.

The king gave a nod, and Chip pressed a button on the machine.

Inside the device's capsule, a beam of light shone onto Jiminy's journal as the book appeared on the monitor.

Eventually, a flood of images leaped out from the book, all from the places they'd visited during their previous travels. It seemed that memories really did remain within the journal.

The data extraction appeared to be going smoothly, until a large number of strange blocks appeared on the monitor. Red geometrical patterns raced along the surface of black cubes, glowing with an eerie light. The images started to disappear behind all the black and red.

"Hey, what's goin' on?" Dale seemed confused, but not particularly concerned.

"Jiminy's journal—I think it's gone completely nuts!" Chip crossed his arms with a worried look.

"Nuts? Where?"

"That's not what I mean!" Chip scolded his easygoing brother, then began hammering away at the keyboard attached to the device. But the monitor was already filled with blocks.

"I don't know what's causing it exactly, but there's something wrong with the worlds inside the journal. And we can't analyze that message for you, either!" Dale said.

Mickey sighed. "Hmm, isn't there something else we can try?"

Gazing up at the monitor, Goofy muttered a suggestion. "Gawrsh, maybe if we could get in there somehow and fix the data, we could figure out what's wrong."

Chip smiled as the lightbulb went off above his head. "Hey, that's it!" he exclaimed. Everyone turned to look at him. "We could look for somebody already in the journal and ask them to explore the worlds and repair the data. That's a great idea, Goofy!"

"Somebody to explore the data from the inside..." Jiminy crossed his arms in thought at Chip's proposal.

Then, Mickey got to his feet as his own idea occurred to him. "And I think we know just the guy to do it! Am I right, fellas?"

There was only person they could think of to call for this:

"Sora!" Donald hopped up and shouted.

"But how...?" Goofy wondered.

"Everything will be fine. Right, Sora?"

Mickey smiled at the monitor.

Sora was sinking into the depths of a deep, deep sea—a sea of data. This record of the boy within the journal both was and was not Sora—a Data-Sora. Still, Sora was Sora in any form.

He opened his eyes.

> *Can you hear me?*
> *Now, step forward. Can you do it?*

He didn't know where the voice was coming from, but Sora stepped forward as he was told.

> *Power sleeps within you. If you give it form—it will give you strength.*

*　　*　　*

He had heard these words before—back in some other time, in some other place. This was the beginning of his journey.

It was time to depart; his adventure was about to unfold.

"We're in business! That takes care of rewriting Sora." Dale cried. Sora's form was displayed clearly within the monitor.

"Rewriting?" Goofy inclined his head, bemused.

"Yep! We rigged it so he can use the Keyblade already. Now he can help us un-glitch all the journal data!" Chip explained.

"This data is a new Sora?"

Goofy tilted his head so far he was starting to lean over. Who was this Sora within the data?

"It means it's a Sora based on everything Jiminy wrote down."

"Are you saying he's not the same Sora we met on our journey before?" This time, Donald was the one with questions.

"Your journey with the real Sora was all recorded into data. So he *is* the Sora from before, just another version," Mickey replied with a smile, but Donald and Goofy still seemed slightly lost.

"An' since he's still Sora, he can help us restore all the worlds to the way they're supposed to be."

As Chip paused in his work for a moment, an alarm sounded from the monitor, and the image distorted.

"Is something wrong?" Mickey asked with concern.

"Could be something gumming up the system."

"Wait here. We'll hop next door and have a look. Be right back!"

Chip and Dale nodded to each other and then dashed from the study. After a moment, the alarm shut off, and Sora could be seen standing in the monitor exactly like before.

"Well, I guess Chip and Dale figured the problem out," said Jiminy with a sigh of relief.

As a sudden question occurred to him, Goofy turned to Mickey. "So, uh, Your Majesty... What is it we're doing, exactly?"

"Oh! Somebody wrote a strange message in Jiminy's journal. And the only way to find out who is by analyzing the book," Mickey answered.

"What does the message say?" Now Donald was the one with questions.

"'Their hurting will be mended when you—'"

Before Mickey could finish, Jiminy hopped up on Mickey's shoulder and pointed at the screen, interrupting him. "Curious..."

"What is it?" Mickey looked at the screen, too.

"Hey! Look at the monitor! What's *he* doing there?!" Donald cried out as he spotted the unexpected figure.

Someone wearing a black coat stood behind Sora.

"Gawrsh, I thought Sora said he was alone in that dream," Goofy commented, equally concerned about the suspicious newcomer.

That person standing there—who were they?

Sora glared angrily at the figure in black. This place was inside the data—or, in a manner of speaking, inside Sora's dreams, but Sora himself didn't know that.

"Who...are *you*?"

The mysterious individual didn't respond to his question but instead began to walk off, following the path that materialized before them.

Listen! Can you hear me? You have to go after him!

As that somehow familiar voice called to him again, Sora took off. The path took him to a light-filled platform, rising up from the gloom just like the first. No one else was there. When Sora tried to continue the chase, two Heartless—Shadows—appeared before him.

*   *   *

Watch out! Heartless! Use your powers!

"Use my what?"

As Sora inclined his head in confusion, a key-shaped sword—a Keyblade—flashed into his hand.

"How did…?"

> *You've gained the power to fight. And this is your power to survive. There will be times you have to fight. Keep your light burning strong.*

Sora could feel the strength welling up within him at those words. He readied his Keyblade and then charged toward the Shadows. Sora swung his Keyblade, and when it struck his foes they vanished in a burst of light. At the same time, a large door appeared in front of him.

> *Now, open the door. Hold out the Keyblade.*

As the voice advised, Sora extended his Keyblade toward the door. A beam of light shot from the point, and the door seemed to swallow the light as it opened.

> *Now, get moving!*

Sora nodded at the voice, then plunged through. For a moment he was blinded, until he realized he was back home on the islands—the Destiny Islands.

"Huh? How'd I get back here?" he mumbled.

Though slightly relieved by the familiar sights and sounds, Sora was a little disappointed. Then he heard the voice once more.

> *Sora.*

*   *   *

"Who's talking to me?" Sora responded, glancing around. He still couldn't find the owner of the voice. It was like the sound was coming from overhead—no, *inside* his head.

Sora, are you okay?

"How do you know my name? Have we met?" Sora replied with a question of his own.

Gee, well, sort of. I'm Mickey. Let's just say I know you, Sora, and Sora knows me. We're good friends.

Not quite sure of what this person calling himself Mickey was getting at, Sora folded his arms and fell into thought.

We've never met, but I know who Mickey is, and we're friends? That doesn't make much sense. You couldn't be friends with someone if you'd never met them before, right? Sora decided to voice his feelings directly. "That…doesn't make any sense."

He heard a small chuckle in response.

You see, I'm from another world and— Gosh, it's a long story. There's this mystery me and my friends are tryin' to solve. But we can't get to your world, so we were hopin' you'd lend a hand.

"I have to solve a mystery?" Sora mulled over the situation. Now he was even more confused.

For starters, this whole thing about different worlds puzzled him. *And the reason Mickey can't get here, even though he can talk to me, is because…uh…*

Well, we're searchin' for an answer somewhere in that world you're in. And you're the only one who can find it.

*   *   *

"Hmm, I don't know what's going on, but are you saying you want me to explore the island?"

> *Yeah, that's it exactly! And if there's anything you need, I'll be right here.*

"Great!"

> *Okay, so the first things we're looking for are "glitches." Anything out of the ordinary.*

Sora shrugged. He had thought this place was as boring as ever when he arrived only a moment ago, but now he could see something *had* changed, and it was plain as day.

The island was littered with what appeared to be strange red-and-black blocks—he had never seen anything like them before.

"Well, that's easy. These blocks! How'd they get on the island?"

Sora gave the block next to him a good chop with his Keyblade, and it vanished without a trace. Maybe he would learn something if he continued to get rid of them.

> *Perfect! That's part of our mystery.*

"All right, then. I'll try asking around!" Sora replied. He spotted Selphie a ways up the beach and ran over to her.

As the boy went, Mickey spoke to him, full of hope:

> *Thanks! And remember, Sora. We might be worlds apart, but just say the word and I'll do my best to guide you. No matter what happens, I'm always with you in spirit.*

CHAPTER 2
Destiny Islands

That's where the whole story began...as did the glitches. And for good reason—because nothing ever happens by chance in our stories. Everything is connected. This is where someone else set off on a journey, too, long ago. Does this world feel small to you, Sora? Or does it feel large? Who will be the one to unravel the secrets of this world—of the Destiny Islands?

Sora took off running toward a girl in a yellow dress, his friend Selphie, who stood by the edge of the water. She was surrounded by the blocks Mickey had asked him to investigate.

"Sora, where have you been?!" Selphie called out to Sora in her usual cheery way. "Would you look at the island? We're up to our ears in blocks!" she complained.

Sora came to a halt. Selphie was just as surprised by the unusual circumstances as he was. Maybe she knew something?

Sora folded his arms and asked her. "Who put 'em here?"

"Nobody! They keep popping up out of thin air!"

So she didn't have any idea, either. This was her first time with these blocks, too.

"We'll be buried alive at this rate. That's if Tidus and Wakka aren't 'six blocks under' already."

Now that she mentioned it, Sora didn't see any of the other faces he usually saw on the island. Meaning he should ask...

"Why? Where'd they go?"

"Down to the beach to investigate."

"Well, that's not far. I'll go see what's up."

Sora hurried down along the sandy shore. Except for the blocks, the island was the same as it always was, with the sound of the waves, the sand crunching pleasantly underfoot, and the great blue sea.

Wakka called out to Sora as he approached. "Hey! Sora! Things are gettin' hairy here, ya? You okay, brudda?" Wakka was a bit older than Sora and the rest of the island regulars, and someone they knew they could always look to for help.

"It's been an interesting day. Where did these blocks come from, Wakka?"

"They just kinda showed up. Before ya know it, they're everywhere. Ya get rid of 'em, and they come right back."

Wakka was apparently in the dark, too, unsurprisingly. He had never seen anything like this before, either.

"I'll go check it out!" Sora declared.

Wakka shrugged uneasily. "You sure?"

"Yeah, wait here," Sora replied with a confident thump on his chest. Mickey had offered to help out, and plus, he had the weird key. Everything would be fine. He turned to rush off down the beach.

"Hey, Sora! While you're at it, do me a favor and check up on Tidus for me?" Wakka shouted.

"Where is he?"

"We split up to investigate. He can't have gone too far, but you know him—he's probably in over his head."

"No worries, I'll bail him out."

"Thanks, brudda!"

Sora had jumped into the task headfirst, but he actually didn't know what the best course of action was. He might as well get started by smashing the blocks while he looked for Tidus—but there were way too many. According to Selphie and Wakka, they would keep coming, too, yet he had to do something.

Sora reflected as he destroyed the blocks scattered around the beach.

It would be impossible to play tag here even if he wanted to; all the obstacles would make it dangerous to run very fast.

"Huh?"

Sora stopped in his tracks as he noticed something.

The pier leading out to the smaller island was missing.

Maybe this was another "glitch," thanks to those blocks. Sora could also see a silhouette that looked like Tidus's out on the islet.

"I guess I'll try heading over there anyway…"

The bridge used to lead from the little seaside shack.

Breaking the blocks in his way with his Keyblade, Sora arrived at the little hut—and when he did, someone wearing a black coat walked by.

This guy…!

It was the one Sora had encountered in that strange place before he returned to the Destiny Islands. He tried to hurry after him, but he was already gone.

"Huh?"

Sora walked around a little in search of him, but no luck.

Suddenly, the world went dim. No—it was like the world was flickering before his eyes. *What is happening…?*

Suddenly, he heard Mickey's voice.

Sora, I'm picking up some kind of signal. Wait, I'm analyzing it and… Yep, no question. There's some kind of invisible door near your position.

Sora drew up short and fell into thought at Mickey's words. "Invisible door? Is that another glitch?"

It just might be. Sora, follow that signal and look around. I think we're finally onto something!

"Got it! I'll look for the door and find that guy," Sora replied, then began his search. Something was off near the entrance to the shack. He'd more or less found what he was looking for, and as soon as he started peering more closely, the air seemed to tear apart to create a hole.

"Whoa! What is that?"

It was too dark for Sora to tell what was inside, but he thought he could see the same red pattern as on those blocks.

* * *

> *Sora, this world is made of data, so everything operates through a program. If you can beat the bugs in the program running this world, everything should return to normal.*

The words coming out of Mickey's mouth left Sora completely confused as he fell into thought.

What's "day-ta"? And "programs"? And "bugs"?

Well, I bet it means there's some bad guys through that hole, and they're messing with whatever keeps this world going.

"I need to go in here and defeat something inside, right?"

> *I'm counting on you, Sora!*

With a nod at Mickey's words, Sora entered the fissure.

Before him was a bizarre space built of square shapes. There were also several of those familiar blocks piled up. They fit right into this otherworldly space, and it was undoubtedly clear that this was the source of the problem.

"All right, bring it on!"

Sora gripped his Keyblade and charged forward. As he did, the same monsters that had first given him the opportunity to wield the key appeared around him. What were they called? Heartless.

Sora swung his Keyblade and wiped out the Heartless exactly as he had done in the past. Were these the "bugs"…?

Once he had done away with all of the Heartless, something resembling a pillar of light rose up in the center of the room.

> *You should be able to return to your regular world from there.*

With a nod at Mickey's explanation, Sora stepped into the glowing pillar.

As soon as the intense light enfolded his body, Sora found himself back on the familiar beach of the Destiny Islands.

Just like before, the blocks were everywhere, and he couldn't see that anything special had changed. The bridge was still missing, too, and he hadn't run into that guy in the black coat.

Feeling a tad deflated, Sora took a step forward—and then the bridge flashed into place in front of him.

Mickey had said that place with all the squares was a "program," right? So maybe he could fix the problems in the real world by getting rid of the "bugs" in that realm of "data."

"Okay, let's keep it up."

Sora ran across the bridge to the islet and called out to Tidus.

"Tidus, there you are! Wakka was worried."

Tidus turned to face Sora, wooden sword in hand.

"Man, did you see that? The missing bridge…it just popped back into existence! And these blocks… Last I checked it's not April Fools'," Tidus ranted, gesturing with his wooden blade.

"Too bad we don't know what's causing all this."

"Heh-heh! Or *do* we?" Tidus crowed, rubbing his nose proudly.

"No way! You figured out where the blocks came from?"

"Well, no…" Tidus's response to Sora's second question sounded a bit more uncertain.

"What do you mean?"

"I found a clue."

"Really?"

"What do *you* think?"

While Sora didn't know exactly what it was, he was sure Tidus really had come across a lead. Lying wasn't Tidus's style, so Sora felt safe trusting his word.

"Okay, well, tell me what it is then."

"You wanna know about the clue I found, you'll just have to earn it."

"All right, you're on!" Sora said, summoning his Keyblade.

"No holding back, now."

Tidus closed the distance between them in a flash.

Sora blocked, then landed several of his own attacks right in a row. Tidus was knocked onto his rump, but he leaped instantly back to his feet and swung his wooden sword again. Sora dodged and whacked him on the shoulder with his Keyblade from behind.

"Oof…" Tidus came to a halt. "I keep forgetting how tough you are." He sat down wearily.

"Just don't forget what you promised."

"Okay, so I saw this stranger walking around the island," Tidus said, his shoulders heaving with each breath. "Don't ya think the timing is a little suspicious? First these blocks show up, and then some weirdo in a black coat?"

A black coat… It has to be that guy!

Sora dismissed his Keyblade and helped Tidus up. "Black coat?" he asked. "You saw that guy?!"

"Over by the waterfall. Then I looked away for one second, and he was gone," Tidus said as he brushed the sand off his pants.

Sora turned toward the falls in question. Speaking of the waterfall, wasn't there a small cave nearby?

"The waterfall. Got it! Thanks, Tidus."

Sora ran back across the bridge to the island, then continued into the cave beside the waterfall.

A cool, damp draft flowed through the interior. The walls were covered with the scribbles and drawings they had all made.

Sora looked around, but he didn't see any black coats—only a big door in the back. *He must have gone through there*, Sora thought, reaching toward it.

The ground suddenly trembled.

"Whoa! Wh-what's…?"

There's a road for the taking if you end our world's aching.

He heard a voice from somewhere—and it wasn't Mickey's? *Who was that?*

The world continued to rumble and shake. At that moment, a brilliant light shone from Sora's Keyblade, engulfing him.

Something similarly strange was taking place on the monitor in Disney Castle.

"Huh? What... What's that bright light?"

"Wak! I can't see a thing!"

The gleam from Sora's Keyblade was so strong that Mickey and everyone else around the computer had to close their eyes against it.

The light flooding from the monitor intensified, as if it would swallow up the entire study.

"Wak?"

Opening his eyes after a moment, Donald surveyed the area. Nothing appeared out of the ordinary.

"Gawrsh, what happened? I'm still seein' stars, a-hyuck!" Goofy peeked between his fingers, but the room looked the same as always.

"Huh?!" Jiminy cried. "Not again... Look at the journal! There's a new entry!"

Another passage had been written in the journal on the monitor.

"'There's a road for the taking if you end our world's aching,'" Mickey read aloud.

Behind him, Donald and Goofy looked at each other.

"What does *that* mean?" Donald asked.

Goofy could only wonder himself. Similarly, Mickey crossed his arms and fell into thought with a serious expression.

"The world is aching?"

What exactly did "the world" refer to? Maybe it meant the world they were seeing on the monitor now was in pain.

"Not just 'the' world. 'Our' world..." Jiminy seemed to have the same questions.

Then Goofy noticed something else. "Huh? Hey, look at the monitor!"

On the screen was Sora, and...

*   *   *

"This world has been connected." In the dim cave, the man in the black coat spoke for the first time.

"Huh? Hey, I've been looking for you!"

"Tied to the ——," he continued, as Sora instinctively readied his Keyblade.

"What?" Sora asked back, unable to hear him clearly. But the man's reply was the very words Sora had just heard in his head.

"There is a road for the taking, if you end our world's aching."

"What 'aches'? Are you talking about the blocks?" Sora asked the man, but it didn't seem like he was going to get the answers he wanted.

"To make this place whole, the Keyhole's the place," the man stated simply, then began to walk away.

"Hey, wait!" Sora started after him, but a large...something rose up in front of him.

What could it be? Was this that "Keyhole"?

Sora, do you read me?

As Sora stopped in his tracks, he could hear Mickey's voice.

"Mickey, I've got something weird here. That guy in black left behind a... Well, it looks like a keyhole."

Hmm, any ideas?

Staring intently at the object that had appeared, Sora replied, "As a matter of fact... What did he say again? 'To make this place whole, the Keyhole's the place.' I think I need to find a way through."

Hmm... Why don't you try the Keyblade? That might do something.

*   *   *

"Of course! I'll give it a shot."

When Sora held out the Keyblade toward the keyhole as Mickey suggested, he heard a *click* like something unlocking, and light washed over him.

Before he knew what had happened, Sora found himself standing in a storm, battered by the wind and rain.

"Whoa! What is this place?"

It was still his home on the Destiny Islands, but the weather here had taken a severe turn for the worse.

Sora! Are you okay?

"For now, anyway. Any idea where this is?" Sora replied, but the palms of his hands were slick with sweat. *These...are my islands, right? But they've been ripped apart...!*

I'm not sure. But I'll tell ya one thing... Whatever's causing the glitches must be in there with you.

"And if I find the cause, I can put the island back to normal?"

Just be careful, Sora. Whatever's in there, it's powerful.

"Right."

As Sora nodded in agreement, the sky split open with a gale-force blast of wind. From the depths of the black sea—an unimaginable sight for someone used to the placid waters of the islands—arose a colossal Heartless. It was a Darkside.

"You're the one causing all this trouble!"

Steeling himself for a fight, Sora charged at the Darkside with his Keyblade in hand.

At the same time, the Darkside brought its fist down onto the ground.

Was it only Sora's imagination, or did that fist resemble the blocks all over the island? Just what was going on here?

When Sora struck the Darkside's fist with his Keyblade, the Heartless stopped moving.

The wind picked up again, hurling Sora into the air.

What was that? Argh, I have to find some way to beat this guy!

As the Darkside resumed its slow, lumbering movements, he noticed the ominous, heart-shaped cavity gaping in its chest.

Fighting down his fear, Sora got to his feet and faced the Darkside once more.

The fists it slammed down were turning into blocks, which in turn came to attack him. Sora dealt with each one using his Keyblade, then landed a series of blows on the inky creature creating them. After he wasn't sure how many strikes, the Darkside let out a howl as the raging sky finally swallowed it. The Destiny Islands were being sucked up into the air, too, along with Sora himself.

He desperately clung to a piece of wood, struggling against the gale, but eventually the vortex in the sky won out. Sora let out a cry as it devoured him, too.

"Do you think Sora's all right?" Mickey wondered uneasily as he watched the monitor.

Jiminy hurriedly began tapping at the attached keyboard with his feet. "Wait, I'm tracking him now."

The journal appeared on the screen yet again.

"Whoa!" Jiminy cried as he saw the book.

"What is it? Donald asked, gazing up at the screen.

"A new entry in the journal!"

There are more hurts than the one you have just undone.

"More hurts than the one…we have just undone?" Goofy read aloud, confused, but then the image on the monitor changed.

"Hey, look!"

What appeared onscreen was the storm on Destiny Islands—except Sora wasn't there.

Instead, Riku was on the islet. And before him was a mysterious man in a brown hood. As the hooded man pointed at Riku, a pitch-black darkness unfurled behind him.

Then the feed cut out.

"Gee, now that can't be right. If the data was repaired, we should be seeing the things that were written inside my journal, right? But what we just saw—that never happened. Or, at least, I never wrote it down," Jiminy said, his voice shaking a little. If the monitor was showing events that Jiminy didn't remember recording, did that mean that the contents of his journal were being rewritten? Or maybe...

"You mean it's showing us stuff you don't know about?" Donald tilted his head in confusion, too.

"Hmm, I wonder what's goin' on inside the journal," Goofy said apprehensively.

Suddenly, a green light began blinking in a corner of the monitor.

"Aha! We've found Sora!" Jiminy announced.

An image expanded outward from the green light, showing them a back alley in a dimly lit town.

CHAPTER 3
Traverse Town

Does it feel like déjà vu? Or more like the start of a new story? What are you dreaming now, I wonder?

A dog licked Sora's face. He was lying unconscious in an alleyway; only a little bit of light was shining around the corner.

"Unh…" Sora opened his bleary eyes slowly, but what he saw was not the ocean of the Destiny Islands nor the sky overhead, but a town he'd never seen before—and a dog.

After he was blown away from the Destiny Islands, he had arrived in Traverse Town. It was a place to live for people who had lost their homes to the "glitches," though they never forgot where they'd come from. There was something peaceful about this place and its neon signs standing out against the night sky.

"What a dream…," Sora muttered, then closed his eyes again. A world like this *had* to be a dream, after all.

But the dog—the king's friend, Pluto—jumped on Sora's stomach.

"Ungh—this isn't a dream!"

Sora stood and rubbed his eyes, then took a look around him. *What is this place…?*

Now that Sora was upright, Pluto looked up at him and wagged his tail happily.

"Oh, boy… Do you know where we are?"

Huh? How did I…? As Sora wondered, Pluto ran on ahead.

Sora followed him into a district paved with brick. It looked like some sort of plaza.

Sora, are you all right?

"Whoa!"

Sora was startled by the voice coming out of nowhere, but then sighed in relief as he remembered that it belonged to Mickey.

He didn't remember much, but this voice was Mickey's, and Mickey was a friend he'd never technically met.

"Mickey, what happened? Where am I?" Sora asked.

Gee, you must've been taken someplace else.

Sora folded his arms and considered Mickey's response. A few things were finally starting to come back to him.

All these weird blocks appeared on my islands, and I used my Keyblade to get rid of them. Then a storm blew me away. What happened after that...?

"Wait! The island! Did I fix it?" Sora asked, thinking Mickey might know.

Yep! All the blocks are gone. You did a great job, Sora.

Then what was that storm all about...? Anyway, the blocks were gone, and that was what mattered. Everyone was probably back on the beach playing as usual.

"So, okay, I'm in a strange town... Why? Is this place full of glitches, too?"

From what he had seen, there weren't any of those odd blocks here.

Could be. Mind taking a look around?

"Sure, I'm on it."

With that, Sora glanced around the plaza and spotted a lone man standing at the top of a nearby flight of stairs. He was maybe middle-aged, with goggles on his head, a brown band around his stomach, and a frown on his face. His arms were crossed, too. Maybe something was bothering him?

Sora ran up the stairs and called out to him.

"Hello there."

"Hnnh? Hey, kid."

The man met Sora's cheerful greeting with an equally spirited one. But he was quick to notice that Sora wasn't a local.

"Haven't seen you 'round before. You new to Traverse Town?"

"The name's Sora! Nice to meet ya."

"Yeah, I'm Cid. This here's my shop." Cid pointed with his chin toward a building with a sign out front identifying it as an accessory shop. He then gave Sora's face another look and stroked his stubble thoughtfully.

"So Sora…don't suppose you ran into the triplets on your way here?"

"Triplets?" Sora tilted his head at Cid's question.

"Yeah, there's three of 'em? *Uno, dos, tres?* They went off to see what's got the town all scrambled, and… Well, they ain't come back."

"Something's wrong with the town?"

"Hoo, I'll say. These weird blocks have popped up everywhich-where. Ya clear 'em out, and they come right on back."

Weird blocks? Maybe they're the same as the ones on my island. This world was having trouble, too, it seemed. Anyway, the blocks weren't here in the plaza…

"But I don't see any blocks right now."

"Oh, you just go for a little walk. You can't miss 'em."

"Okay, I will," Sora replied. He turned away from Cid, then began to run off. He knew every square inch of the Destiny Islands, but this town would be full of unfamiliar places. Finding them would be fun.

"Hey!" Cid called.

Sora stopped and turned around.

"While you're takin' in the town, keep an eye out for the triplets, yeah?"

"Sure. What are their names?"

If these triplets were out looking into the glitches, he might learn something by talking to them.

"Well, there's Huey—he's the feller in red. Dewey wears blue, and Louie's decked out in green."

"Huey, Dewey, Louie. Got it. I'll take a look."

"Attaboy. You got any questions, just ask around town."

"Will do. See ya later, Cid!"

And with that, Sora's search began. There were two large gateways in the square—they would be a good place start. He ran down the stairs and headed for the door on the left, but it wouldn't open.

Maybe the Keyblade will do the trick? He held it out toward the door, but it didn't respond at all. No light or anything.

Sora let out a small sigh, then tried asking a man who was standing next to the door.

"Hey, does this door not open?"

The man replied with a troubled look on his face. "The door to the Third District won't budge. I'd go and find out what's wrong, but I'm no match for all those Heartless."

"That's okay. I can take care of 'em."

Apparently, this door that wouldn't open hid some sort of secret.

"Really? But… Well, if you say so. You'll have to go through the Second District to get to the Third. Take the north door."

"So I guess this is the First District?"

"Yes indeed."

"Thanks for filling me in!"

Sora then retraced the path he had just taken and headed north behind Cid's shop. The blocks hadn't been in the plaza, but there were some back here. Destroying the blocks as he proceeded, Sora reached the end of the path and a big wooden door like the previous one. It opened easily with a light push.

Sora peeked through it to see rows of buildings with a different feel from the First District's. Whereas everything in the First District had been made of brick, here it was all about flagstones. The red-and-black blocks everywhere were the one thing they had in common.

How am I supposed to get to the Third District?

In the distance was a clocktower with a stained glass window. That might be a good place to start. Sora set off at a trot.

"Heeelp!"

As Sora reached the front of the clocktower, he heard a small cry. Looking for the source, he saw atop a block a boy dressed in red with a hat of the same color.

And before him were the Heartless.

"He's in trouble! I've got to help him."

Sora took his Keyblade in hand and charged. At least there weren't many. He swung his Keyblade and defeated the Heartless one after the other.

Once he was sure they were all gone, Sora jumped onto the block and spoke to the boy. "Are you okay, uh...?" *He's wearing red, so...*

"I'm gonna guess you're Huey?"

"That's me! Me and the guys are trying to figure out what's clogging the town with blocks!"

This was definitely one of the triplets Cid had asked him to find. Were they not investigating together?

"You mean you and... Dewey and Louie, was it? Where are they?"

"I dunno. We got separated. They musta gone to check the alleyway."

"Got it. I'll go take a look." Sora started to run off, but then stopped. *Wait, where is the alleyway?*

Huey noticed and called out behind him. "Follow me!"

"Thank you!"

Huey took the lead to show Sora the way.

"Y-yikes!" But then he stopped in his tracks with a yelp as a pack of Heartless appeared, and they looked tougher than the ones Sora had just fought.

"Get back! I'll handle this." Sora stepped in front of Huey to protect him, then faced the Heartless. There were way more of them than before!

He still managed to take them down, though the battle left him out of breath, and he turned back toward Huey.

The boy had been watching fearfully from behind cover, but once he was sure the Heartless were gone, he ran up to Sora with such enthusiasm that Sora almost expected to get a hug.

Relieved, Huey looked up at Sora. "Wow, you're strong," he said.

"You go back to Cid's shop, Huey. I'll find Dewey and Louie."

"Okay." Huey wasn't too keen on the idea of going off on his own anymore after seeing those Heartless. "Oh yeah! Here, you can have this!"

The boy offered what appeared to be a glowing piece of…something to Sora.

"Wow, it's a… What is it?"

"I found it while I was investigating. Pretty cool the way it sparkles, huh?"

While the glimmer certainly did catch the eye, Sora couldn't even begin to guess what it was. It could be some junk for all he knew.

"Yeah, umm… Thanks! Just what I've always wanted…"

"Anyway, I'm goin' back to Cid's. You can get into the alleyway from beside the fountain!"

Sora looked over at where Huey was pointing and saw the fountain near the gate he had come through a short while ago from the First District. Next to it was a door.

"Anyway… Next stop, the alleyway!"

Sora hurried over to the fountain, then turned and opened the door to the alley. Along the backstreet was a small canal—probably connected to the fountain.

"Hello? Anybody there?"

He suddenly heard a voice coming from somewhere, but there was no sign of its owner. *Maybe it came from above…?* Sora looked upward, but all he could see was the underside of a balcony. As he walked ahead a bit, his path was cut off by Heartless. There sure were a lot of them around here.

Suddenly, he heard the voice again.

"Hey, over here!"

Yeah, it was definitely coming from above—so whoever was calling out to him was on the balcony?

After Sora did away with the Heartless, he climbed up the blocks scattered around the alleyway and reached one of the balconies. On the next one over was a boy dressed in blue.

"Whew, thanks! I thought they'd get me for sure!"

"No problem, um… Let's see, blue… Dewey, right? I'm Sora. You okay?"

"Sure am! I couldn't get down because of all the Heartless!" Dewey replied loudly, looking at the street below with relief.

"Well, you should get back to Cid's place while you can."

"Oh, let me give you something for helping me out." Dewey shoved his hand in his back pocket. "So you'll never believe what I found while I was out inv— Huh? It's gone!"

With a small hop of alarm, the boy began searching the balcony.

"What's gone?"

"The thing! Gee, I musta dropped it somewhere in the Second District… I gotta go find it!"

Dewey leaped down from the balcony in a panic and dashed toward the door to the Second District.

"Hey, wait! Where are you—?"

Sora jumped down, too, and went after him. Upon entering the Second District, he saw Dewey on all fours in front of the fountain searching for something.

"Hmm, something that shiny oughtta be easy to spot…"

"Hey! Don't run off like that. It's dangerous."

"Aw, please. What are you afraid of, monsters?" Dewey retorted with a smile. Well, this place *had* been crawling with enemies when Sora saved Huey only a little while ago.

"Still can't find it? What did you—?"

"Urk! Heartless!" Dewey shouted with a leap before Sora could finish his question. Another pack had arrived.

"Dewey! Get to safety!" Sora ordered, readying his Keyblade.

The Heartless were fierce this time, but Sora still managed to beat them.

"I told you it's dangerous," Sora scolded Dewey. He was a little miffed now.

"But I want you to see the thing I found!"

That's nice and all, but it's too risky to hunt for it with so many Heartless around. "Dewey, go back to Cid's. I mean it!"

"Aww! But Sora, I can't go back empty-handed! Just let me look a little longer."

"Oh brother… All right, but stay out of trouble until I get back."

As Sora gave up trying to stop him, Dewey dropped to all fours and resumed his frantic search for whatever he'd lost. His white tail feathers waggled in the air.

"What exactly are you looking for?"

"…I found it!" Dewey shouted and stood up.

"Well, that's great!"

In his hand was a mysterious shining shard. "See how pretty it is when it catches the light? I want you to have it, Sora."

Dewey held the glowing item out to Sora happily. *Wait, this looks familiar…?*

Sora removed the gift from Huey from his pocket. They were shaped quite similarly, but not exactly the same.

"Hey, cool! I wonder if they fit together," Dewey commented as he peered into Sora's hand.

"Actually… Yeah, if I stick this like this…"

Sora put the two shards together. They did fit perfectly, but it still wasn't obvious what they were shards *of.*

"Whoa! Do ya think they're supposed to make something?" Dewey asked curiously.

"Could be… But look. We're still missing some pieces."

Maybe they would be able to figure out what it was if they had all the parts.

"Then let's go hunt 'em down!" Dewey hopped happily, ready to go on another treasure hunt, but Sora grabbed him by his blue shirt and stopped him short.

"Uh, did you forget about what just happened? You're going back to Cid's shop, where it's safe."

"Aww! But I wanna go with you!"

"No *buts*. I'll bring the pieces by when I'm done. Now get those legs in gear."

"Right. Legs in gear, I promise."

Dewey lowered his head meekly and started trudging away, but something didn't seem right. No, Sora knew exactly what he was up to. He would do the same thing in Dewey's shoes.

"Not so fast!" Sora caught hold of that blue shirt again. "Cid's shop is the other way, buster."

"B-but I know a shortcut!" Dewey shook his head vigorously.

"Uh-huh. I better go with you."

"Aww, phooey…"

Sora took Dewey by the hand and began walking back to the First District. The right way.

Dewey looked up at Sora and said while they walked, "You're pretty tough, huh?"

"Not really. I've got a friend who's even tougher."

Actually, what did *happen to Riku…?*

"My uncle's strong, too, but he's got nothin' on you."

"Your uncle… You mean Cid?"

"Nope! Cid's only looking after us. Oh hey, there he is!"

As soon as he spotted the man in question, Dewey shook off Sora's hand and scampered away.

"Dewey! You all right?"

"I'm fine, Cid," Dewey replied cheerily.

Huey was next to Cid. "Gee whiz! Where were ya?" he asked, slightly annoyed.

"The alleyway behind the Second District," Dewey answered.

"Was Louie with you?"

"What? I thought he was with you!" Dewey shook his head dejectedly at Huey's question.

Louie was the last of the triplets.

"Might be he's in the Third District," Cid said worriedly and crossed his arms. "Sorry, Sora—think you could go have a gander?"

"Sure, I don't mind. Actually, I've got something to hunt for myself now," Sora said with a nod.

"Yeah? What's that?"

"You ever seen one of these?" Sora showed Cid the pieces he had gotten from the boys.

"Well, uh, sure! That there's a…a, uh… Nope, no clue."

"We found 'em!" the boys chorused.

Cid held the fragments up to the sky and squinted at them with one eye closed.

"The other pieces have gotta be around town somewhere," Dewey exclaimed with a leap.

"What happens when you put 'em all together?" Cid was still looking intently at them.

"Who knows? Something cool, I bet!"

"Yeah!"

Huey and Dewey both sounded very confident.

"I guess we'll find out," said Sora. "Let's see what I turn up while I look for Louie."

Cid returned the fragments, then folded his arms again and nodded. "Thanks, Sora."

"Leave it to me!"

Sora returned to the Second District.

"Huh?"

The red-and-black blocks were in different places than they were earlier. They'd walled off some areas before; maybe now he could reach them.

Sora explored the Second District and found a newly opened pathway. It would probably take him to the Third District.

"All right, let's do this!"

The Heartless in his way were stubborn, but Sora's Keyblade took them down. He hurried to the Third District.

This neighborhood was full of bright neon lights, very different from the Second District or the First.

"Louie! Are you here? Looouieee!"

He called and called; there was no sign of the boy. Maybe he wasn't here…?

That was when a figure soundlessly appeared before him—wearing a familiar black coat.

"Huh? Hey!" Sora brought his Keyblade up, ready to fight, but the man in the black coat didn't move. "All right, 'fess up! These glitches are your doing!" he shouted again, but the man in the black coat said nothing and strode away.

"Hey! I'm talkin' to you!"

He had entered the Second District. Sora followed him back down the narrow street and into the plaza of the Second District, but a strange sight greeted him there.

The sky didn't look like the sky.

Where the stars should have been was a black canvas threaded with red lights, just like on the blocks. What's more, the clocktower on the far side was enveloped in an uncanny green light.

"What's going on here?" Sora muttered as he headed to the clocktower.

"Whoa, what?! This building… It's flat as a pancake!"

What Sora found wasn't the clocktower, but something that looked more like a stage prop of the clocktower.

"Is somebody there? Heeey!" someone was shouting urgently.

"Louie?! Where are you?"

"Um, can I get back to you on that? All I know is that I was standing on top of a building…"

So when the building got distorted, Louie vanished.

Now that Sora thought about it, the bridge on the island had disappeared, too... This could be one of the glitches.

Which meant that there should be another fissure in this world that could take him to that alternate space. If Sora took out the bugs or whatever inside like he did on the island, he should be able to find Louie.

After some thorough searching, a hole—a System Sector—opened in the wall, exactly like the other one had before.

"Okay, hang in there, Louie!"

Sora plunged into the opening.

"This sure brings back memories," Donald said quietly as he watched the monitor.

"Sure does...," Goofy replied.

"That's where we met Sora for the first time."

"And Aerith and Yuffie, and then Leon... I wonder how they're all doing?"

The two of them reminisced fondly.

Though there were no longer any records of their journey in Jiminy's first journal due to the events of Castle Oblivion, everyone who lived through the events could still remember them.

Just as memories could be recalled, maybe the records they'd discovered in the journal after converting it to data would recover over time.

"This is where you two met Sora, huh?" Mickey commented, as thoughtful as the other two.

"That's got me thinkin', Your Majesty. When we data-fied everything in the journal, all the entries were still there. So the Pluto who woke Sora up came from the data, didn't he?" Goofy inclined his head as he thought.

"What do you mean?"

"Well, shouldn't we all have data versions in there, too?"

"Hmm...I wonder... Jiminy, what do you think?" Mickey crossed his arms and turned to Jiminy.

"I still don't quite understand how this world works, either. Those blocks won't let us get a good look at the entries. I'm guessin' the worlds in the data are incomplete—broken into pieces. What a mystery..."

"Hmm...," Mickey mused, looking down.

"Wak! I'm sure Sora can fix it, though!" Donald said, hopping up just like his nephews. If one thing was for sure, it was that this Data-Sora, born from records of the real version, was indeed Sora. It didn't really matter whether he was data or real.

"You're right. If anyone can get to the bottom of this, it's Sora."

And with that, the four of them returned their attention to the monitor.

Sora eradicated the bugs within the sector—the Heartless—and returned to the Second District.

Everything was back to normal.

"Hello? Anybody down there?"

He heard a shout from above that sounded like Louie. He was probably up on the clocktower.

Sora made his way up the scattered blocks and found a boy in a green cap—Louie.

"You all right?"

"Yeah, thanks to you!" Louie launched himself at Sora and grabbed his leg in relief.

"Good. Let's get you back to Cid's."

Sora picked Louie up in his arms and leaped down to the ground.

"What happened?" the boy asked anxiously when Sora set him down.

"I don't really know, either. Oh! Louie… Have you seen anything like this?" Sora showed Louie the pieces he had gotten from Huey and Dewey.

"Huh? Hey, yeah! I've got one, too. Check it out!" the boy replied, then produced a glowing fragment just like the others from his pocket.

"See if it fits with the pieces I've got." Sora put all three together.

"Whoa, it sure does! But look." Louie sounded disappointed. It seemed they were still missing a segment, but at least now they could more or less tell what it was supposed to be. That meant only one piece remained.

"Whaddaya think it's supposed to be? A keyhole?"

Louie regarded the pieces with his head to the side.

"Keyhole?" The word reminded Sora that he'd seen a keyhole that glowed like this on the Destiny Islands.

"What's wrong?"

"Oh, nothing. Sorry. Let's head back to Cid's."

Sora took Louie's hand and started walking away.

But when they opened the door to the First District, Sora found himself face-to-face with the man in the black coat, which shifted in the breeze.

"Louie, get back! No—run! Go right to Cid's!"

Sora stepped in front of the boy protectively and got into a fighting stance with his Keyblade. Cid's place wasn't far.

"Okay. Be careful!"

Once he was sure he heard Louie running off, Sora stared down the figure in black. "I hope you're happy with all the trouble your glitches have caused!"

In response to Sora's accusation, the man in the black coat tossed something over to him.

"What're you—?" Sora quickly scooped it up. "Wait… Is this…?"

It was another glowing piece. Sora looked up hurriedly, but the man in black had already vanished in that brief moment.

"Huh?!"

Sora pulled the other pieces from his pocket, and then they floated into the air, the four pieces combining into a keyhole.

"I knew it. It's the same as before."

Sora, can you hear me?

Then he heard Mickey's voice. Sora decided to ask him.

"Mickey, listen to this. You remember that Keyhole from the island? I've found another one. If this all works the same as last time…"

You think the source of the glitches might be waiting inside.

"Exactly. And if I go through the Keyhole and defeat it…"

The town might turn back to normal… You'd do that, Sora?

"We've come this far. Leave it to me!"

Sora held his blade toward the Keyhole floating in midair. Light shot from his Keyblade into it, and a door opened with the sound of a lock opening.

"Okay, here goes!"

The moment he ran through the door, Sora tumbled head over heels.

"What just happened?! Is this Traverse Town?" Sora yelled, plummeting so fast it was like something was sucking him downward.

Sora, careful! I'm reading enemies right near you!

Sora landed while Mickey was talking, and right in front of him, he heard the sound of metal scraping against metal. With a great rumble, a giant Heartless shaped like a suit of armor—Guard Armor—revealed itself.

If I beat him, those glitches will be history!

"All right, let's get this party started!"

Guard Armor abruptly jumped into the air, ready to stomp on Sora.

Dodging the attack, Sora circled behind the Heartless and swung his Keyblade at its back.

That stopped Guard Armor in its tracks. It rotated its great head, searching for him.

"Heh-heh! Over here!" Sora taunted, and Guard Armor responded with a sudden laser beam from its face. Sora rolled out of the way and positioned himself behind the Heartless once more before striking with his Keyblade.

"Time to put an end to this!"

With a mighty leap, Sora brought down his Keyblade, and Guard Armor came to a halt. After a moment, its body fell to the ground in pieces that vanished into light.

"I did it!" Sora struck a macho pose and grinned.

The Keyhole spit him out and sent him tumbling into the First District. The blocks were still there, even though he thought he'd defeated their source.

"Why are the blocks still here? Didn't I get rid of the enemy controlling them?" he muttered.

Mickey answered his question.

> *You did. Now you just need to sweep up. Use your power, Sora, and end the glitches here once and for all.*

"My power?"

Sora stared at his hand. *What power...?*

> *Uh-huh. A power that's yours and yours alone. Use the Keyblade to lock the Keyhole for good!*

Sora raised his head and saw the Keyhole still hovering there. So he merely needed to close it? "Right! Here goes."

*   *   *

That should be the end of the blocks in town. Nice work, Sora! You've solved this world's mysteries.

Sora nodded and held his Keyblade up toward the Keyhole again. This time, he heard the lock close, and the door blinked out of existence without a trace.

Good, the town was back to normal now. Still, Sora was bothered by man in the black coat.

I guess he really is the one messing up the worlds...?

The moment Sora closed the Keyhole, the monitor distorted with static.

"What's happening?" Donald asked apprehensively.

With a hand on his hat to keep it in place, Jiminy did a tiny hop. "It's another new entry!"

At Jiminy's shout of surprise, Mickey and the others all looked at the journal inside the digitizer.

There are more hurts than the one you have just undone.

"Hmm... It looks to me like a new message gets added each time a world inside the journal is repaired," Mickey commented as he thought.

"Yeah! Just like before. Which means..." Donald looked up at the monitor.

Riku had appeared onscreen after Sora had fixed the Destiny Islands. Jiminy had not made any record of that event, so maybe they would see something this time, too.

After a few moments, the display showed Sora shaking hands with Donald and then Goofy in Traverse Town, not long after they had first met. The real Donald and Goofy had been talking about that first meeting earlier.

"Gawrsh! I remember that," Goofy commented.

"Does that mean that we've appeared inside the journal now that the world is fixed?" Donald asked.

But the viewpoint of the image on the screen shifted slightly to show Pluto in what looked like an alleyway.

He headed deeper into the alley, sniffing at a scent. Beyond was one of the inky black portals they had encountered many times during their second journey—a Corridor of Darkness. The feed cut out right as Pluto dashed toward it.

"That's funny. We were there... Was Pluto with us?"

"Well, I sure didn't write anything like that in the journal." Jiminy was as puzzled as Donald was.

Something unrecorded had appeared on the monitor. There was still no telling whether it was an event that had actually taken place or not.

"Hey, do you fellas think that maybe the journal is trying to tell us something?" Goofy wondered. What exactly was going on with this little book?

Just then, something very strange happened.

"Wak!" Donald cried.

Something had appeared in the room with them—a group of Heartless.

"Here, in the castle? But how?" Jiminy exclaimed in a panic. Mickey leaped from his chair and brandished his Keyblade. In a single flash, the Heartless were dispatched.

"We gotta check the rest of the castle now!"

Donald and Goofy followed Mickey as he rushed to the door. But...

"It won't open!"

They pounded on the door, but it didn't budge. Chip and Dale, as well as Minnie, Daisy, and Pluto would all be on the other side.

"Hey! Hello?! Anybody out there?"

No response.

"This is not our day," said Jiminy quietly.

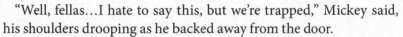

"Well, fellas…I hate to say this, but we're trapped," Mickey said, his shoulders drooping as he backed away from the door.

"We're what?! But there could be more Heartless roaming the castle," said Donald in a worried tone. Was Daisy safe?

Just then, an alarm indicating another new entry came from the computer.

Everyone quickly checked the monitor and saw yet another entry in Jiminy's journal.

Undo the hurt to unbar the way.

"What does that mean?"

Jiminy put a hand to his head in confusion. All these short new entries—what did they mean?

"'Undo the hurt to unbar the way'?" Mickey read the message aloud.

"Gawrsh, we're tryin'. It said we've already undone some of it, right?" Goofy said, thinking with his arms crossed.

"Well then, we'll just have to keep going, repairing the journal's data as fast as we can," Mickey replied.

Donald and Goofy shared a glance.

Suddenly, the view on the monitor changed again to show Sora.

"Your Majesty," Jiminy said, turning back to Mickey, "I think Sora might've reached the next world."

"But we gotta do something about the castle!" Donald pleaded.

"I'm as worried as you are, Donald, but right now our best hope is fixing up the journal."

With that, Mickey turned to watch Sora on the screen. Donald and the others did the same, trusting that their king was right.

CHAPTER 4
Wonderland

Our memories are connected, like links in a chain. Those same chains are what bind us all together. I don't destroy memories, I just undo the links and rearrange them. That connection—that's what's important, Sora. Both in our memories, and in our bonds with each other.

Before he knew it, Sora was standing somewhere new.

He had been in Traverse Town only a moment ago, had only closed his eyes for a second, and then he was standing here. Sora looked around, completely confused as to what had transpired.

He was in a magnificently tended garden, surrounded by bushes trimmed to form neat hedge walls with crisp square corners. The scenery was lovely—except for all the blocks.

Sora, do you read me?

"Mickey, what is going on? Where'd the town go? I was there just a second ago, wasn't I?" Sora asked, relieved to hear Mickey's voice.

I'm sorry, Sora. I don't know what's goin' on. Eliminating bugs in one world must open a road to the next.
"Undo the hurt to unbar the way"…

Sora took a moment to contemplate what Mickey had said. It had to be the bugs that were causing the hurt.

"Wait, so that thing I clobbered inside the Keyhole… That was a 'bug'? So then…these blocks must be bugs, too, right?"

Sora looked around as he spoke. They were ruining such a beautiful garden. It was impossible to take in the view without something in the way.

*   *   *

That's right—or at least bugs are what caused them. So far, the major bugs seem to have been hiding inside Keyholes. You'll probably need to find this world's Keyhole, too.

Another road would open if he got rid of the bugs, and then he would probably get tossed into a different world.

A world he'd never been to before. He was starting to enjoy the idea of seeing so many new things.

"Sign me up! I've always wanted to see other worlds. Just point me at those bugs!"

Ha-ha! That's the spirit!

Sora gave an enthusiastic nod at Mickey's encouragement. Plus, opening those new roads would help people in trouble.

"Someone! Help!"

Suddenly, he heard a girl's scream.

Sora hurriedly took his Keyblade in hand and ran toward the sound. A girl with blond hair in a blue dress and apron darted out from behind a block and over to him in fear.

"Help! Please!"

"What's the matter?"

Heartless were in hot pursuit behind the girl.

"Right. Get back, I'll take care of 'em!" Sora called, then charged toward the Heartless. They fought back, but with the help of his Keyblade and a little magic, Sora made short work of them.

"Whew! Good riddance." The girl smiled at Sora.

"You okay?" Sora asked, dismissing his Keyblade.

"Why yes! Thank you, er… I'm sorry, have we met?" The girl tilted her head curiously.

"Oh, I'm Sora. What's your name?"

"Well, it's…it's…" The girl seemed to be thinking very hard about Sora's question.

"What's the matter?"

"Oh, it's hopeless! I simply can't remember a thing!" She shook her head.

What does she mean? She can't remember anything?

Just then, a cat appeared suddenly before the girl and Sora—well, its head did, to be precise. It was an uncanny purple with a very large mouth.

"You could say her mind's like me—a bit fuzzy."

"Huh?! What are you saying? She has amnesia?"

Instead of answering Sora's question, the floating head kept talking. "Gesundheit! No, silly. I mean what the miss has misplaced lies literally littered about the palace. Yes, her memories—oh, and everyone else's, too. The place has become quite buggy, you see—or maybe you don't."

As the cat explained, the rest of its purple-and-pink-striped body gradually faded into view.

"Bugs? That's what Mickey said… So the bugs have caused everybody's memory to go all funny? I better find the Keyhole quick," Sora said.

The girl looked at him in surprise. "Keyhole? Was it a very large Keyhole?"

"Yes! You saw it? Where?" he asked, but the girl lapsed into thought again.

"Hmm… Ooh, I can't seem to recall…," she mumbled in distress.

"Poor dear," said the cat. "What's to remember with her memories dismembered?" The body disappeared again until it was only a head bouncing strangely back and forth. "No, to get the girl thinking, what you need is an Inkling." The cat's tail came back and pointed at something sparkling near a block in a corner of the garden.

"An Inkling? What'll that do?"

"Don't look at me! It's not as though *I* have an Inkling! But if you find one, this whole mess will surely be forgotten. Or is it remembered?"

With those parting words, the Cheshire Cat vanished.

"H-hey! Sheesh…"

The cat wasn't coming back anytime soon. *Anyway, let's go grab that Inkling.*

"Wait here."

Sora ran over to the corner of the garden, jumped atop the blocks, and picked up the sparkly object.

ALICE was written on what appeared to be a small shard. *Maybe that's her name…? Well, only one way to find out.*

Sora leaped down from the blocks and made his way back to the girl.

"Ohh, whatever was my name? It's on the tip of my tongue…"

"It's Alice," Sora told her, offering her the glowing Inkling.

The light disappeared into her, and then the girl—Alice—smiled.

"Yes, of course! I'm Alice!"

"Hey, that's great! Your memory's back! So, Alice, where did you see the Keyhole?"

"Well, let me think. It sort of…glowed, as I recall," Alice mused.

If Sora could just find the Keyhole, he would be able to get rid of the disturbances around here.

"Yep, yep, that's the one! Where was it?"

"Hmm, well that's… Oh dear. I suppose I'm still a bit foggy about the details."

Then, the Cheshire Cat reappeared in front of Sora and the troubled Alice. "But the fog that's bogging her could be unclogging with the right memory jogging."

If what the cat said was true, Alice's slowly recovering memory would also help her remember where the Keyhole was.

"But where can I find more Inklings?" Sora asked.

The cat flipped over into a handstand. Sora had never seen a cat doing a handstand before. Well, he'd never seen a cat that could fade in and out of existence, either.

"Oh, this way, that way, and in-between ways. And don't remember—in blocked ways, too." The Cheshire Cat spun about in the air.

"Okay, sit tight, Alice. I'll be back with more stuff to remind you."

"Thank you." Alice nodded somewhat uneasily.

"Ah, careful now. Mind you find the right reminders. Alice's Inklings lie strewn about. But then, so do everyone else's! The question is: which are remind-hers, and which are remind-thems?"

With that, the cat dissolved into thin air again like a puff of smoke.

So everyone else's memories were messed up, too. Well, if Sora tracked down all the memories, Alice's would be included.

"Guess I'll have to sort it all out."

As Sora was about to walk away, the man in the black coat appeared before him.

"That's right. Sort it out and end the hurt. Our world still aches, and your next road still awaits."

"What are you after? And how do I figure into it?!"

The man didn't even deign to answer Sora's question, and instead he disappeared just as suddenly as the Cheshire Cat had.

Sora still had no idea what the guy wanted. Right now, though, he needed to track down Alice's memories.

He left the garden to find yet another, but here the hedges formed a maze. As he made his way along, Sora found his path blocked by a card soldier with a heart-shaped spearhead at the ready.

"You there. What are you doing?"

"Me? Oh I was looking for, um…for something I lost."

"Well, you may kindly look elsewhere! These gardens are the property of Her Majesty the Queen of Hearts. Wander about, lad, and I'm afraid it's off with your head."

In that case, Sora would just have to sneak by without drawing attention.

He pretended to turn back, but as soon as he was out of the soldier's sight he snuck by along a different route that kept him hidden behind the hedge walls.

There were roses growing here and there around the garden. They smelled wonderful, but the stems were full of prickly, painful thorns.

"Huh? Hey, is that…?"

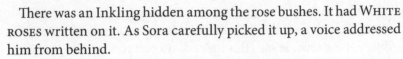

There was an Inkling hidden among the rose bushes. It had WHITE ROSES written on it. As Sora carefully picked it up, a voice addressed him from behind.

"Hey!"

"Ack! They saw me!" Sora ran off in a panic, the heart-card soldier chasing after him.

He managed to lose his pursuer only to arrive at a dead end with another card soldier standing there. This one was a spade.

"I've made a real blunder this time... 'Off with his head!' the Queen of Hearts will say. Look at me! I've worked so hard, I'm covered in dirt! And for what?! I got it all wrong. What was my mistake?"

So this soldier had amnesia, too. True, he *was* covered in dirt... and the only work around here was gardening. And Sora had only one other Inkling as to why that was.

"Maybe...white roses?"

"Yes! I planted white roses instead of red ones! Quick! Do you know where I can find some paint? Here, you can have this as thanks for helping me remember."

The card soldier gave Sora the Inkling "Queen of Hearts."

I sure hope the queen won't lop off that soldier's head... Sora continued onward until he reached a gate immediately before the dead end.

The moment he stepped through, he yelped. "What—What happened?! I'm tiny!"

This place was nothing like the garden where he had just been. It was an ordinary room with a tidy arrangement of furniture, perfectly normal except for one thing: everything in the room was oddly large. Apparently, Sora had shrunk.

Then, the Cheshire Cat appeared. For some reason, he always showed up to chat when strangeness was afoot. "Being little makes for big trouble, hmm? Especially with them around. What to do, what to do?" With those cryptic words, the cat vanished again.

"Hey! D-don't just leave!" *What did he mean, "them"?*

Out of nowhere, a huge Heartless appeared in front of him.

"Agh! Giant Heartless!" Sora cried out, startled by its size. The

Heartless had grown as much as he had shrunk. Something this big would be all the harder to take down. "You won't beat me, though!"

Sora was able to defeat the Heartless somehow. Thankfully it had been just the one. He doubted he would be so lucky if Heartless of this size came at him in numbers.

With these doubts in his mind, Sora went as far as the table in the center of the room, only for the Cheshire Cat to show himself again. Now there were two small bottles—one red, one blue—standing on the table. What were they?

"Surprised to see me? Here's a little something for rising to the challenge. After all the commotion, you might like this little potion." Then he was gone again.

Sora was left with an Inkling and two bottles of what the Cheshire Cat had called "potion." The glimmering shard had CHESHIRE CAT written on it.

Alice should already know that name. As for the two bottles, the red one had a picture of a tree growing larger on it, whereas the blue one showed a tree shrinking.

"I guess that means…this one." Sora took the red bottle and drained it all in one go. He got bigger, just as he'd thought. Now he should be able to get around here without too much trouble.

Sora searched the room and came upon on a small door. The doorknob was askew, though.

"What a weird-looking doorknob," Sora muttered…and then the doorknob twitched. "Agh!"

"'Weird'? Impertinent! Of the two of us, I would say *you* look pretty odd for a doorknob."

"It talks?!"

As Sora recoiled in shock, the doorknob let out a big yawn.

"I'd just fallen into the nicest nap, and then the whole world turned on its side! Mmm… Do take care. You never know when another twist of fate might be at your door."

A twist of fate at his door…? That had to be a System Sector. "Must be another bug. Don't worry, I'll find a way to put things right again."

"Please do… I'm so tired…"

Sora walked around the room again, and before long he found another fissure in the air.

"Okay, in I go!"

Sora entered the System Sector.

"Inklings…and memories," Jiminy said softly as he observed the monitor.

"Something on your mind, Jiminy?" Mickey asked.

The cricket tilted his head thoughtfully. "Do you remember what Naminé was called in that report?"

"…A memory witch!" Donald shouted before Mickey could respond. During their second journey, they had discovered Ansem's secret report—the report of Ansem the Wise—and it had described Naminé.

Naminé was a witch who controlled the memories of others.

"Somethin's been bothering me."

Jiminy pulled the other journal from his pocket.

"In your second journal?" Goofy asked, looking at Jiminy's hands.

"The journal that's givin' us all the trouble is the first one. The one that says *Thank Naminé*. The second journal is perfectly fine."

Jiminy flipped through the pages of the book in question. Among its various entries were some details on Naminé.

"Are you sayin' she might have something to do with the glitches?" Mickey asked.

"I wouldn't say it's definitive…but I do have a hunch that she's connected in some way," Jiminy replied.

Mickey crossed his arms in thought for a moment, but soon raised his head.

"Anyway, let's keep watching," he said, returning his attention to the monitor.

When Sora returned from the System Sector, he was greeted by a huge yawn from the doorknob.

"That should make it a little quieter around here."

"Mmm, finally, some peace and quiet. I'll be getting back to that nap now. Take this as a token of thanks."

The doorknob gave Sora an Inkling. It had WATCH written on it.

"Okay, sweet dreams."

"Good night."

Bidding farewell to the doorknob, whose eyes were already closed, Sora left the room from a side entrance.

"What's with this place?"

It was another garden, just as immaculately tended as the others. In the center was a big table, on top of which Sora saw the leftovers of an apparently recent party.

Was someone there?

"Hey, anybody here?!" Sora called out, but he was answered by the arrival of the worst kind of uninvited guests: Heartless. "No, not *you*!"

Sora slashed with his Keyblade and dodged the attacks, but one Heartless managed to avoid him. It landed on the table and began kicking dishes everywhere.

"No, not there! Over here!" Sora called, and the creature came after him again. "Okay, party's over!" He did away with the Heartless in a flash and then grinned.

But there was still something beneath the table, he could tell.

"Come on out!"

"Ooh, I really must be going. I'm already late, late, late!"

"Whoa!"

The mysterious guest popped out from his hiding spot: a white rabbit wearing glasses.

"Um, h-hello. What were you doing under the table?"

"Why, hiding of course! Those shadows showed up and… Oh me, oh my," the rabbit muttered, pushing up his glasses.

"What, the Heartless? I took care of them. It's safe now!" Sora announced.

The rabbit peered intently at Sora, then tilted his head to one side. "Yes, that's well and good, but I'm late for a very important…something. Whatever was it?"

So this rabbit had lost his memory, too.

"Sorry, I don't remember. I just know I was going somewhere in a hurry." The rabbit stood with his arms crossed in thought.

Sora decided to ask him a question. "Listen, do you know anything about a girl named Alice?"

"Hmm, Alice, you say? And a girl? Yes, perhaps I do…"

"Really? That's great! I—"

"But then, perhaps I don't. I simply can't recall."

They wouldn't get anywhere like this. Maybe he would need to find the rabbit's memories, too.

"All I remember is, I glanced at something and knew I was dreadfully late! But what?"

What could that be? What do you look at when you're in a hurry?

Sora recalled the Inkling he had received from the doorknob a bit earlier. "Was it this, do you think?" The glowing Inkling Sora held out read WATCH.

"Yes, of course! I saw the time and knew I'd be late to the trial!"

As soon as he accepted the Inkling, the rabbit dashed off before Sora could get a word in edgewise.

And when the rabbit was gone, another glowing object was left behind—the Inkling "White Rabbit."

Maybe this was Alice's memory. Sora dashed off to deliver the Inklings to her.

* * *

Alice was waiting nervously in the middle of the garden.

"Hey, Alice. I'm back," Sora called.

"Do you think you could help me get my memories un-fuddled?"

"Sure!" Sora replied, then took out the three shards he had obtained.

"I was in a field of flowers, as I recall… Then I saw someone and began to follow them."

Sora had three Inklings on him: "White Rabbit," "Cheshire Cat," and "Queen of Hearts." The Cheshire Cat would be hard to follow since he liked to appear and disappear at random, and the Queen of Hearts lopped off people's heads, so she probably wouldn't be spending her time in a field of flowers. That left only one.

"It has to be the White Rabbit."

Sora gave Alice the "White Rabbit" Inkling.

She smiled. "Yes, it was a White Rabbit, and he seemed in an awful hurry. I followed him into a burrow, then fell down a peculiar hole. That's how I got here."

The White Rabbit had definitely left Sora in a hurry, too.

"Do you remember what happened next, Alice?"

"I tried to ask someone how to get home. Oh, who was it?"

Sora still had the "Cheshire Cat" and "Queen of Hearts" left. It was the Cheshire Cat who had told him about Inklings in the first place. So, the answer here had to be…

"The Cheshire Cat, right?" Sora gave her the Inkling.

"That's right, the Cheshire Cat. And he suggested I visit the castle of…someone important."

Only one left.

"That would be the Queen of Hearts."

"Precisely! And while I was trying to ask the Queen of Hearts how to get home… Oh! There in her court is where I saw the Keyhole!" Alice smiled happily. She had remembered everything.

"I'm glad you got your memory back, Alice."

"Yes, thanks to you. So what shall we do? Go and have a look?"

"You bet!"

With that, Sora and Alice set off for the queen's castle.

Just then—the man in the black coat appeared behind them, watching them go.

"…The truth lies through the Keyhole. And with it, true memories…," he murmured quietly, then vanished.

Sora and Alice continued walking toward the castle without noticing or turning back.

The "queen's castle" was a rather strange place. It was less a castle and more an audience chamber in a garden, where the queen sat atop her tall throne and the rabbit waited obediently off to one side.

The moment she spotted Sora and Alice, the queen pointed her heart scepter and shouted, "Who are you?!"

"Oh, don't mind us. We only need to have a quick look around." Paying no mind to the short-tempered queen, Alice began to march right in.

"Stop where you are! This is *my* garden, and only I decide who gets to look around or asquare or any other shape. Is that clear?"

"Yes. Well, no… It's just that we're in a hurry, you see…"

Perhaps Alice was in a bit too much of a hurry. As she stopped, the queen examined her appraisingly, then announced her judgment. "Hmph, a likely story! I demand that you both stand trial immediately!"

"What?!" Sora exclaimed. Why were they suddenly on trial?!

"Oh please, Your Majesty! We haven't done a thing!" Alice shouted.

"Aha! A lie if I've ever heard one. More proof that you're the thieves who made off with my memory!"

I didn't know the queen lost her memory, too. I could have looked around for more Inklings…

"Hey!" he cried defensively. "That's not our fault! It's the bugs that took your— Urk."

"So… That's how you did it! You and your army of insects!"

Bugs was a bad choice of word. The queen pointed her scepter at Sora and Alice, then raised her other hand.

"Please, be reasonable," Alice argued. "You have no evidence!"

"I most certainly do! For one, I've decided you're guilty!" the queen spat coldly.

She was speaking complete nonsense, and before anyone could even respond, the queen delivered her verdict.

"Guards! Off with their heads!"

A large circle of card soldiers formed around Sora and Alice.

"Oh no! Run, Sora!"

"Wait, Alice. Where's the Keyhole? You said you saw it."

"Yes, over there! Inside that birdcage!"

Alice pointed out a small cage, covered with a cloth, beside the queen's throne.

While it was quite a ways up, Sora spied a wheel next to it. Spinning that would probably lower the cage.

"Thanks!"

"Sora," Alice called as he started to run off, "where are you—?"

He paused. He would probably lose his chance to get to the Keyhole if they ran away here, and they couldn't afford that. "I have to get to the Keyhole, and this could be my only chance. Don't worry about me. Go on, run!"

"But—"

"I'll be fine. Trust me."

"Well…all right. But don't let them catch you."

Once he was sure Alice had gotten away, Sora made a beeline for the wheel. But the card soldiers got in his way. As he did battle with several of them, Sora figured out that five or six blows from his Keyblade were enough to wear them out.

"He's getting away! After him, you imbeciles!" the queen roared furiously.

With a sidelong glance her way, Sora fought his way through the endless waves of soldiers before finally reaching the wheel. He gave it a big spin.

Just as he'd thought, the birdcage came down.

"Don't let him get away!" the Queen of Hearts shouted. Near her, Sora removed the cloth from the birdcage.

There it was! The Keyhole. Like before, Sora held out his Keyblade.

A light shot from the tip and into the Keyhole, and a door appeared.

As the queen howled and raged, Sora plunged inside.

"Whoa! Where am I now?!" Sora yelped.

Beyond the door was nothing he'd ever seen before. The earth and the sky were upside down, and there appeared a huge Heartless with long arms and legs that attacked with bizarre movements—Trickmaster.

The monster swung its flaming clubs at him in an inscrutable dance, but Sora managed to keep away from them and wore it down with spell after spell from his Keyblade.

But the weirdness didn't stop there. Suddenly, the world tilted on its side so that the ceiling was on the right and the floor was on the left. It was getting hard to make sense of anything anymore.

Apparently, the world would rotate every so often.

"Oh, come on!"

Sora needed to bring this fight to an end fast. Otherwise, he really was going to fall prey to his opponent's games.

Changing his strategy a bit, Sora sprang off the wall—or was it the ceiling now?—toward Trickmaster.

Then, with all his strength, Sora swiftly struck the Heartless in the torso with his Keyblade. The blow felt solid under his hands.

Trickmaster's arms, soft as cloth, were the core of a crafty offense that had given Sora a lot of trouble—but finally, they fell still.

And when they did, Trickmaster turned into a flash of light and vanished.

Eventually, the world spun back right way up.

"Now everyone's memories should be back to normal!"

Sora twirled his Keyblade, then rested it on his shoulder with a grin.

"That's another world repaired," Mickey commented, watching Sora on the monitor.

"Look, just as we thought! Another line has appeared in my journal! 'There are more hurts than the one you have just undone,'" said Jiminy, watching the journal in the digitizer. He turned back toward Mickey, but Donald and Goofy didn't seem very happy.

"That doesn't sound good."

"Uh...fellas... The door's still locked."

The door to the study wasn't any closer to being open than it was before. They were still trapped. Goofy had tried the door, but it didn't budge. They had hoped fixing the glitches in the data world would restore the problems in this world, too, but apparently it would take more than that.

"'Undo the hurt to unbar the way.' Other worlds in the journal must still need our help," said Mickey with chagrin.

Exactly how many hurts were there in the worlds within the journal? And what did they need to do to get out of this room?

"So, will Sora be heading to a new world?" Jiminy looked up at the monitor again. On the screen was Sora and... "Look! It's him!" he cried.

"What does he want this time?" Donald was equally surprised.

Sora was glaring at the figure in the black coat.

"I've got you now!" Sora took up his Keyblade, ready for a fight, but the man in the black coat didn't move. "I want some answers! Somebody's behind these glitches. Is it you or not?" he asked.

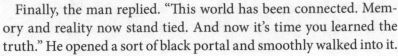

Finally, the man replied. "This world has been connected. Memory and reality now stand tied. And now it's time you learned the truth." He opened a sort of black portal and smoothly walked into it.

"Hey! Get back here!"

Sora ran in after him.

"How're we gonna find out who he is?" Jiminy muttered nervously.

"What if he's Organization XIII?" asked Donald grimly.

Organization XIII was known for its members' black coats. But the Organization had been wiped out, as far as they knew. The worlds inside the computer were worlds within memories—so maybe the Organization existed there as data?

"Don't worry. Sora will catch him. Then we'll know for sure," Mickey assured them somberly. Suddenly, they heard a noise from outside the room.

"Who's there?" Donald ran up to the door. Someone was on the other side.

"Chip and Dale musta come back to rescue us!" Goofy cried happily.

And then the door opened.

"Wak!"

Donald fell onto his backside in shock when he saw who it was.

Sora, with his Keyblade at the ready.

"You're here?!" Mickey sprang up from his chair and ran over to Sora.

"That voice... Mickey? Is that you?" Clearly confused, Sora put away his Keyblade.

"What happened?"

"I was just...following that guy, and..."

Before Sora could continue, the screen abruptly filled with static.

"Majesty! There, on the monitor!" Jiminy shouted.

Everyone looked up at the same time. After less than a second, what appeared was—Mickey's back. And Donald, Goofy, and Jiminy were there, too.

"What's going on here?" Mickey muttered, but then turned as he sensed someone else was there behind him.

Suddenly, standing next to Sora was—the man in the black coat.

"Wak!"

"A-hyuck!"

As Donald and Goofy yelped in surprise, the man's hood vanished like an image fading from a screen.

And the one standing before them was…

"Riku?!" everyone cried at once.

All along, the man in the black coat had been Riku.

But the boy shook his head quietly. "Sorry. Not quite. Much like Sora there, I'm just zeroes and ones that look like somebody you know," he slowly explained. Sora stared at him with his mouth agape.

Riku started typing on the keyboard, and Jiminy's journal appeared.

"Memories used to fill Jiminy's journal—but when they were pulled apart and then stitched back together, bugs appeared. It was these bugs that kept the book from being completely restored. Of all the vessels to protect the data, I was chosen from the journal's pages. The full set of memories was transferred inside me to shield them from corruption."

Everyone seemed confused by his explanation. A vessel to shield memories?

Looking at all their clueless faces, Riku chuckled and then continued. "So, in a way…what I really am is Jiminy's journal."

"You're my journal?" Jiminy asked in shock.

So this Riku *was* Riku, but also not Riku? A vessel that stored the set of memories within the journal? For a vessel, though, he sure seemed to have a will, a purpose—a mind. Did it come from Riku himself? Or was it the "mind" of the scattered memories inside him? Or maybe it was even the mind of someone connected to the memories within the journal…?

As Jiminy tried to make sense of it, Riku kept typing until the words written in the journal appeared on the monitor.

* * *

Their hurting will be mended when you return to end it.

"I took the liberty of importing all of you to help solve the mystery of this entry."

"'Imported'? Where?" Donald had no idea what that meant. He cocked his head to one side quizzically.

"You really haven't noticed?" Riku asked, slightly exasperated.

Mickey looked up at the monitor and saw the image of himself do the same.

Meaning...

"Are you saying...?"

"Yes, we're inside the journal."

Riku nodded with one final keystroke.

Your Majesty! Your Majesty!
If you can hear us, please say something!

That was Chip and Dale.

"Chip? Dale?" Mickey replied to the voices coming from the air. Exactly like Sora when he responded to Mickey's calls.

We finally got through!
The room was empty when we came back, and we've been searching the data for you ever since!

As Chip and Dale explained, Goofy crossed his arms and fell into thought.

"Well, if Sora's here with us, and Chip and Dale are out there lookin' in, then..."

"Then we really are inside the datascape, just like Riku said," Mickey finished, nodding at Goofy.

Riku was standing quietly next to them, arms folded. Mickey

turned to him and asked, "Maybe you can tell us—is there any way for us to get back home?"

Before Riku could answer, an alarm sounded.

It was the same noise Mickey and the others had heard way back at the beginning when they turned on the analysis device.

Oh no!
Someone's trying to break into the data from the outside!

Hearing Chip and Dale's cries, Riku hurriedly turned toward the keyboard.

A whole slew of the red-and-black blocks had appeared on the monitor.

"A hacker! If that's true, then there won't be any way out for you."

Riku hammered away at the keyboard in an attempt to fix it, but the blocks on the screen wouldn't go away.

You have to escape before—

The chipmunks' cries broke off.

"Chip? Dale!" Mickey called, but there was no reply.

"No luck. The link from here to the real world has been totally cut."

Riku shook his head, and his hands fell still on the keys.

"How 'bout some *good* news?" Donald looked up at Riku apprehensively.

"If we repair that link, a new pathway should open," Riku replied. "Of course, that's if these bugs weren't around."

That did little to cheer up anyone.

Suddenly, Sora spoke up. "I don't understand it all, but basically, this means you guys can't go home, right? Okay. Then I'll go bash the bugs for you."

"You will?!" Donald hugged Sora's legs happily.

"That's swell!" Goofy smiled, too.

Then, Mickey held out his hand. "Sora. That's another one we owe ya," he said gratefully.

Sora accepted the handshake. "Who says we're keeping score? We're all friends, right?"

It was such a straightforward response, and Mickey and the others shared a look. Sora would always be Sora.

"Right. See you." Sora swiftly turned to leave the room, ready to run off—but then turned back and scratched his head.

"…Actually, where am I supposed to go?"

"Sorry, Sora. I'll open the path to a world that's still bugged."

Riku tapped a few keys, and a dark portal opened just like the one that had brought Sora here from Alice's world.

"Okay, bye for real this time!"

Sora took a deep breath and set off again.

CHAPTER 5
Olympus Coliseum

Who do you think made this special world? And what do you think was necessary to enter it?

I want to see you, Sora. There's so much I have to tell you. This is all so that you can be ready. The world is full of hurt—the real bugs. What do you think is behind it?

The moment Sora left Mickey's study, everything was different—the air, the smells, even the colors.

He found himself in another unfamiliar world, just as suddenly as before. He was standing in a place that resembled a plaza, and before him was a huge stone edifice. Was it a temple or something?

Sora.

Normally, it would be Mickey's voice coming from the air, but not this time.

"Is that…? Riku, is that you?" Sora called excitedly.

He heard a little chuckle from Riku before he asked a question of his own.

How's it looking?

"So far, things have been pretty quiet."

As far as Sora could tell from looking about him, there was no sign of any Heartless or anything else out of the ordinary. No blocks here, either.

Well, don't expect them to stay that way. One of the bugs interfering with the link is in Olympus Coliseum—I'm sure of it. And you know where it'll be hiding. Find the Keyhole. If my findings are right, that'll take you to the world's core. Get

*rid of whatever's harming the core, and the rest of the bugs
will be purged with it.*

"Yep, that's what me and Mickey figured, too. Okay, be back before
you can say 'bug spray.'" Sora started walking toward the entrance
of the stone structure.

Okay, be careful.

As Riku cautioned him, Sora entered the temple. The first thing he
saw was a small bearded satyr—Phil—pacing back and forth.

"Ugh, this is a nightmare. What's taking him so long?"

There they were, in front of Phil. Several of the increasingly familiar blocks had formed a pile that was impossible to get around.

"What's taking so long?" Sora asked.

"It's the champ! First these stupid blocks and…and now he's gone
and… And why am I telling this to a squirt like you?" Phil gave Sora
the barest of glances and then resumed his pacing.

"First of all, the name's Sora. Second of all, you've gotta tell *somebody*, right?" Sora retorted, somewhat peevishly.

Squirt? Come on. I mean, I guess I am *a kid, but I'm also the only
one who can fix these glitches.*

Phil gave Sora a long look. "…Hmm." After a moment of thought,
he slowly continued. "Good point. Well, just look around! I got
nothin' against new architecture, but these things gotta go! And you
should see the *inside*. The champ—Hercules—went in to investigate
ages ago…"

Phil crossed his arms and didn't elaborate further.

"What, he hasn't come back? That's terrible! I'd better get in there
and see what's up," Sora urged.

There was no telling what could happen on a world with glitches.

But Phil gave a vehement shake of his head. "No dice, kid. The
entrance is blocked… But then, that's obvious, right? It'd take some
kind of hero to get in, but all I see is me and some…kid?"

Without waiting for the satyr to finish, Sora summoned his Keyblade and did away with the blocks in a flash.

"How did…?"

Phil was stunned.

And so was Sora. He had found the Keyhole.

Usually, he only discovered a Keyhole after running willy-nilly and wearing himself out, but this one showed up right off the bat.

What's more, beyond the Keyhole should be a powerful Heartless—a bug. What exactly was going on with this world? At any rate, this was probably the way into the Coliseum.

"This is the Keyhole. Does it lead into the Coliseum? One way to find out!"

"Look, I dunno if— No, maybe you do have what it takes. The name's Phil. Just be careful in there. Getting in is one thing, kid. Getting out is another," Phil said with concern.

Sora replied with a grin. "I'll be careful, Phil."

"Just remember the secret to success. Four words: One…victory… at a…time!"

Four words…? That sounded more like five, but whatever.

"Uh… Thanks. Be back in no time."

Sora then held out his Keyblade toward the Keyhole. The blade's light shot into the hole, and a door opened where it had once been. Sora charged through it.

Hercules raised his head, noticing something strange.

It felt like someone was there—but maybe it was merely his mind playing tricks on him. He couldn't imagine many people were capable of making it here.

He had managed to get inside the Coliseum, which was all well and good, but for some reason, it had become a maze where it was impossible to advance without breaking those blocks. What was worse, it was teeming with monsters. *This is worse than Phil's training*, Hercules thought with a smirk. "I hope I can find some way to fix the Coliseum…," he muttered. He punched the wall of blocks in front of him, and it crumbled to reveal a new path.

Okay, time to get moving!

Meanwhile, deep within the labyrinth was a lone, sinister-looking man with sickly, pale-blue skin—Hades, the Lord of the Dead. The blue fire of his hair was even eerier than his complexion.

"Hmph. I guess they'll let anyone in here," he muttered, stroking his chin as he noticed Sora in the maze. "Sorry to burst your baklava, kid, but you picked the wrong labyrinth to get lost in. If some hero-shmero can't find his way out, where's that put you?"

Hades's rant continued.

"Now, back to stuff I care about: Hercules! This time, I'm kicking his heroic heinie straight into the Underworld! But, ahem, first I think I'll watch the pipsqueak squirm a bit. Oh, I'm going to enjoy this…"

Hades vanished in a puff of smoke.

Sora came to a halt as he saw what lay beyond the door. Whatever this was, it didn't look like a coliseum. In fact, the series of small rooms reminded him more of a maze. The Heartless were everywhere.

This was the first time he had found a world's Keyhole in the first place he looked and his first time encountering such a complicated labyrinth. The glitch here might be more severe than any of the ones he had faced before.

Finding Hercules fast seemed like the best course of action.

Sora, can you still hear me?

* * *

The voice from the air wasn't Riku's this time, but Mickey's.

"Sure can, Mickey! You should see the glitches in here," Sora replied, stopping in his tracks.

Yep, the bug readings are off the charts. It almost looks like... Gosh, Sora. It looks like the Coliseum's turned into a labyrinth.

"Then there's no time to waste. We need to find out what's causing all this harm," Sora declared, almost as much to himself as to Mickey.

How strong would the bugs in here need to be to suddenly transform a world into a labyrinth?

I agree, but Sora... This time, the glitches are affecting you, too.

"Then I'll just have to improvise," Sora replied with a grin and a thump to his chest.

That was when a Heartless decided to jump him from nearby.

"Whoa!"

Sora swiftly defended himself with his Keyblade, then fell to his knees in exhaustion. The Heartless in this maze were quite strong. Still, he wasn't ready to throw in the towel yet. Sora stood up and squared off against them.

After observing Sora for a bit, Hades rubbed his chin and groaned softly.

"Hmph, pretty tough for a half-pint."

It bothered him—the little brat had a special power, and it reminded him of the other kid's, too. That power... Just who was he? He might be worthless on his own, but Hades got the feeling that might not be the case if he teamed up with Hercules.

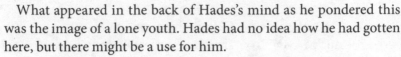

What appeared in the back of Hades's mind as he pondered this was the image of a lone youth. Hades had no idea how he had gotten here, but there might be a use for him.

"Heh-heh…"

Hades chuckled and vanished in a puff of smoke.

"Hmm, dead end."

Sora had been making his way deeper and deeper into the labyrinth, fighting Heartless every step of the way. He'd searched this last room high and low, but he couldn't find a new path anywhere even after all the blocks and Heartless were gone.

There was no way forward. All he saw were brown walls.

Maybe I'll find a new passage if I turn around. Sora was about to double back when he heard a loud noise from behind him.

He turned back to find that the wall blocking the way forward had collapsed, and emerging from the breach was a brawny young man. When Sora imagined a hero, this was the kind of guy who came to mind.

"Whoa! How'd you do that? Let me guess… Hercules?" Sora asked, running up to the young man.

"Um, that's right. And you are…?" Hercules asked back, mildly confused.

"Finally! I—I mean Sora. It's about time I found you! Phil asked me to check up on you."

"Phil sent you in *here*? I'm not sure whether to say 'thanks' or 'sorry.' Anyway, nice to meet you, Sora. I guess Phil mentioned I'm the Coliseum champ. I trained with him to become a true hero." Hercules flashed his white teeth in a smile. "But you have to be pretty tough yourself if you made it this far on your own!"

"Heh-heh! Well, my Keyblade helped," Sora replied with a grin. He linked his hands behind his head. "So you're in here working solo, too?"

Hercules frowned. "Yeah. I'm trying to figure out what turned the Coliseum into…this." He fell into thought.

As he looked up at Hercules, Sora's expression grew serious, as well. He got the feeling he could talk to a hero about the trouble that had befallen this world. "Me too. Somebody's trying to harm this world…and I'm pretty sure the culprit's in here with us," he explained.

"What do you mean 'harm'?" Hercules's expression turned even grimmer.

"The blocks. The maze. Everything funny going on is connected to one villain."

"I see… But, uh, how do you know that?"

"Oh, err… It's kind of a long story. Sorry, I can't really…" Hercules probably wouldn't understand what "bugs" were. Sora hadn't even understood at first, and he wasn't confident he did now. Still, he could make sure Hercules would get the point. "Say, Herc… Any idea who our villain is? Who would want to harm the world?"

Hercules crossed his arms and gave it some thought. "Hmm… Well, one snake definitely slithers to mind," he responded with a suspicious look. "Hades, Lord of the Dead. He's gotta be wrapped up in this somehow."

Just hearing "Lord of the Dead" gave Sora a bad feeling about the guy. "Okay, let's go pay him a little visit!"

"I guess that's the fastest way to find out. He's not around here, I can tell you that much. So, Sora. As long as we're both in here, what do you say we team up?"

Hercules's expression softened, and he extended his right hand. As long as they were working toward the same end, fighting as a team would be way better.

"Sure, if you don't mind!"

Sora grinned and gripped Herc's hand firmly, and the hero responded in kind. The hero's palm was large and strong.

"'Course not!" Hercules said cheerfully. But in the next instant, his expression grew stern again. The reason was obvious—more

Heartless. "Especially now that we've got company. C'mon, Sora. Let's sort these guys out and take back the Coliseum!"

Hercules rushed toward a cluster of Heartless and swung his fist at them. The wind pressure of the blow was enough to finish off one of the monsters without the punch connecting. Even unarmed, he had incredible strength.

"Nice work, hero!"

Sora swiped underneath his nose, then gripped his Keyblade and brought it down on a Heartless. He could take these guys out, too.

"You're not half bad, either! At this rate, we'll be done by dinner!" Hercules called as he turned to his young companion. Sora had never fought alongside anyone else before, so this was kind of fun.

And with that, the two of them proceeded into the depths of the labyrinth, defeating Heartless along the way.

"Heh-heh…"

Hades's ominous laughter rang throughout the maze. His aura was so sinister that the air itself around him turned dark.

"Buy a clue, losers. As if fighting me will make the big, bad labyrinth go away. Okay, you're on deck. Go put those chumps out of my misery."

A blond-haired youth was standing in front of Hades. He held a large sword as tall as he was, and a red cape hung from his shoulders. A single black wing sprouted from his back.

This young man's name was Cloud. "And the road to the next world will open if I defeat them?" Cloud asked Hades.

"Exactamundo, Spike. And this is your big chance to see what makes a hero tick. That's what you're after, right?" It was anyone's guess whether Cloud believed it or not; he said nothing.

"Look, I know, I get it. In the past, you've always come up short when it counted. But with a true hero's strength—still with me? Well, buddy boy, let's just say you'll never come up short again. Now, go and show Hercules who can really go the distance." Hades was speaking quickly, goading him along.

But Cloud's expression remained unchanged. "Let's get one thing clear." Hades's right eyebrow rose up in displeasure at Cloud's chilly reply. "I'm not doing this for you. This is my fight. You stay out of it."

With that, Cloud turned his back on Hades with a swirl of his cape and walked away.

Looking up at Hercules, Sora thought about how this might not have gone so well had he been on his own. He wouldn't have given up, of course, but being all alone in here would definitely have been disheartening.

"Man, heroes are cool."

"Where did that come from? And hey, you're pretty cool yourself," Hercules said with a laugh.

"Hmm, I dunno about that."

"I'm sure you'll be even stronger than me someday, Sora."

"Yeah, I wish," Sora said with a smile, then swung his Keyblade and destroyed a block.

"Well, for one thing, you're better at breaking those blocks than I am."

They were almost enjoying themselves as they bantered back and forth. They could keep this up forever, it seemed—but just then, a gust of wind blew before them.

"Are you the hero Hercules?"

The wind brought with it a young man with blond hair—Cloud.

"Who are you?"

Sora immediately shifted into position, ready for battle. Their opponent readied his giant sword.

"To you...a problem," he said softly. "Show me you've got a good reason to fight...and we'll see how it stacks up against mine."

Without any warning, Cloud's sword flashed out mercilessly. Sora barely managed to block the blow with his Keyblade.

Reacting swiftly, Hercules threw a punch at Cloud.

"Urgh!"

Knocked backward for the moment, Cloud recovered his balance while searching for an opening in his two foes.

The intense battle continued for some time. The youth's swordsmanship was so fierce it was impossible for them to attack. *I dunno if I could do this alone*, Sora thought. *But with the two of us…*

After trading several blows with Cloud, the duo fell into sync and began to see an opening in their opponent's defenses.

The next clash would decide the battle.

Cloud sprang from the ground and went for Hercules. Instead of moving away, Hercules instead took a step toward Cloud, linked his hands together, and swung them toward the youth's shoulder. Sora chose the same moment to chop at Cloud's torso with his Keyblade.

"How about that!" Hercules shouted as Cloud fell to his knees.

"So what he said about you is true," Cloud said quietly through ragged breaths.

"Just who are you?"

"Cloud. And I'm no friend of heroes."

Glaring at the two of them, Cloud stood and brought his sword into position.

"Hey, what did we ever do to—?"

Before Sora could finish his question, a ball of intense, pale light shot toward them from off to the side.

It was too sudden. With no time to dodge, Sora couldn't help but close his eyes.

"Nngh!"

Sora opened his eyes fearfully to find that Cloud had bravely offered his body to protect the two of them.

"Tsk. Missed."

Hades stepped out of a puff of strange smoke with a furious scowl on his face.

"Hades! I said this was my fight! Stay out of it!" Cloud shouted angrily.

"Please. This stopped being about you, like, ages ago…okay?" Hades remarked with a disinterested shrug.

"What?" Cloud growled.

"Oh, sure, you *could* have been useful. I mean, hello? I don't lie to chumps like you unless I'm gonna get good mileage. All you had to do was distract Irk-ules long enough for me to mangle his moussaka. But nooo!" Before Hades could get deeper into his laundry list of complaints, Sora jabbed his Keyblade at him.

"All right, admit it! Are you the guy who did this to the Coliseum?"

"Oh, I see, pick on the guy with ambitions to rule the world. *Bzzt*, wrong!" Hades retorted with a little grin.

"It wasn't you?" Hercules exclaimed in disbelief. He was still braced for a fight.

"Sorry, Wonder Boy, but I'm not the only pine cone in your pita. This maze has another keeper. But hey, I'm a fair sort of god. I'll stay out of your way. Why work when I can just sit back, relax, and watch you all wither away to dust?"

With that, Hades turned away.

"Get back here!"

"So long, Spike. Go find a bucket and kick it."

Cloud started after him, but Hades disappeared in a burst of smoke right before his eyes.

"Nice guy." Sora said with a sigh.

Next to him, a grim-faced Cloud was still staring at the spot where Hades had disappeared.

"So I've been tricked…," he murmured, then began to walk away.

"Hey, wait!" Hercules called for him to stop.

"Forget this ever happened." Cloud vanished into the labyrinth without even turning back.

"What's his problem?" Sora said with annoyance as he watched the youth go.

"He's just another victim of Hades's dirty schemes," Hercules reassured Sora gently.

"That doesn't explain why his attitude stinks," Sora complained with a frown. *He comes in here and attacks us out of the blue, and then he leaves just like that. Shouldn't he have at least said "thanks"? Or "I'm sorry"?*

"...Nobody's perfect? Anyways, if Hades isn't our culprit, then that's a problem."

Now that Hercules had pointed out the real issue, Sora's displeasure with Cloud was finally beginning to cool. He crossed his arms in contemplation. "Yeah, we can't get out of here until we find the real villain."

"Guess it's back to square one, then."

As Sora and Hercules resumed their adventure, heading even deeper into the maze...

"Hey, isn't that...?"

The duo recognized Cloud in the distance, hemmed in by a circle of Heartless.

Oh, him again, Sora thought. Still, he couldn't stop himself from checking to make sure he was okay.

Cloud's massive sword was whirling around in a fury. He was outnumbered, though, and appeared to be having a rough go of it.

"Cloud! Are you okay?!"

"Hold on! We'll be right—"

Sora and Hercules attempted to move closer, but Cloud shouted back at them, "Leave me! You two get out of here!"

"But Cloud! We can't just..." Hercules hesitated and shared a glance with Sora.

"I dug myself into this hole and almost dragged you in with me. Now I'll pay for what I've done."

"That's crazy talk!" Sora shouted, and before he knew it, he was in the midst of Cloud and the Heartless. He just couldn't leave the youth on his own.

"Can't you two take a hint?" When Cloud tried to refuse the help, Sora answered by hurling his Keyblade into one of Heartless. Similarly, Hercules stood beside Sora and batted away the monsters who came his way.

"Why are you helping me? Pity?" Cloud asked behind Sora.

Sora turned toward him and caught his Keyblade as it returned to him. "Yeesh," he retorted. "Would it hurt for ya to let us do you one favor?"

Without waiting for an answer, Sora lunged forward again into the pack of Heartless.

"C'mon, this time you're fighting alongside us!" Hercules called. He followed Sora's lead and slammed his fist into a Heartless. Cloud quickly closed the distance to join them, slamming his enormous blade into the throng of monsters. As two or three Heartless vanished at a time, Sora and Hercules grinned.

They fought on as a trio, and between them, they took down at least ten Heartless.

"No matter what I do, I'm always letting somebody down."

The moment all monsters on the scene were gone, Cloud turned away from Sora and Herc, ready to wander off on his own again.

"Cloud, wait. Whaddaya say we work together?" Hercules suggested.

Cloud stopped. "Why? I attacked you." He still had his back to them.

"But only because Hades tricked you, right?"

"Doesn't matter. I've got no right to join you. I'm not strong enough."

Hercules wasn't about to give up. He was about press the matter further, but Cloud didn't seem to have any intention of joining forces with them.

"Ugh!" Sora stamped his foot at Cloud and his behavior, then took a step forward and grabbed his cape. Cloud whirled around to find Sora staring up at him. "We're not asking if you're qualified for the job. What do you *want* to do?"

"Huh?"

While Cloud appeared to have his reasons for being so cold, none of that mattered here. It was way too dangerous to go through this maze alone, and if Cloud had his mind set on taking down Hades, then it made sense to work together.

"If you're dead set against it, we won't force you. But it beats spending all your time digging around for excuses." Cloud took a sharp breath, and Sora kept up the pressure. "If you've lost your way, just pick a direction and walk! You might catch sight of something along the way, something that'll put you back on course."

Hercules followed up Sora's angry rebuke with one that was gentler. "You protected us when Hades attacked, and I'll bet you didn't even think about it. That was the real you. Somebody strong that we can trust."

For a fraction of a second, Cloud's expression softened into an embarrassed smile, but he quickly looked down as if to hide it and gave a small shake of his head.

"It wasn't strength, it was... Heh, guess I *am* making excuses. Man, you guys are gonna be sorry..."

"Then you're in?" Sora joyfully replied.

Cloud raised his head and brushed Sora's hand off his cape. "Don't get the wrong idea. I need to find a way out of here, same as you. I'm just tagging along until then."

Cloud strode off without waiting another moment, but his posture wasn't nearly as bullheaded as before.

"Whatever, tough guy," Sora retorted under his breath as he followed behind.

Hercules fell into step alongside him. "Hey, we can't all be people persons," he said with a smile. "Some folks are better at finding strength on the inside."

"Hmph. I don't get it."

"It might still be a little over your head."

"And what's that supposed to mean?"

As Sora and Hercules went back and forth, Cloud turned around and called, "Speed it up, you two."

"Oh, yeah? And why do you think we slowed down in the first place, wise guy?" Sora shot back before giving Cloud a body slam from behind.

"…Ow."

"Serves ya right."

"Okay, guys, I think playtime's over," Hercules said in a serious tone and came to a halt. Before them was a large door.

"That doesn't belong here, huh?" Sora asked, his voice low and tense.

"I doubt we'll find anything pleasant behind it." Cloud sounded nervous.

The air from behind the door was extremely ominous.

"Okay, let's go!" Hercules shared a determined nod with Sora and Cloud, then opened the door.

On the other side they found a dull, dank underground chamber. They could see a cell enclosed by iron bars directly ahead. Something was very wrong about the air drifting from the darkness within. It smelled foul, almost like raw meat.

"Whatever we're up against, it's close," Hercules said, and the moment he did, the bars began to rise with an eerie metallic screech.

"Grrr…" A few seconds later, the deep growl of a beast sounded from the gloom.

"What was that…?" Sora frowned at the sudden chill in the air.

"I think we're about to find out."

"Yeah. Ain't no gettin' off the train we're on now…"

Sora and the others passed under the iron bars, then edged forward a bit at a time, staying on guard, until the silhouette of an enormous beast slowly came into view. With a great roar, a black dog with three heads stepped into view…

"Oh no. That's Cerberus, guardian of the Underworld! Well…sort of. There's something wrong with him!"

Hercules lowered his center of gravity, bracing for a fight. A low growl rumbled from Cerberus as saliva dripped from the beast's jaws.

"Cerberus? There's a name I've heard before." Cloud readied his sword.

"This is the worst I've ever seen the glitches... He's the one. He's what's messing up this world!"

Sora, too, brandished his Keyblade.

Cerberus pounced.

"Listen, Sora. You wanna be a hero one day, remember this: No matter how bad things look, where you need a friend to be there, he'll be there!"

"A friend?"

"I'm talking about you and Cloud! We've been fighting side by side, so you're my buddies now. I believe in you. Careful, here he comes!"

Cerberus lunged forward, and one of the beast's heads bit down ferociously on Hercules's shoulder.

"Urgh!!"

"Hercules!"

Cloud slashed upward at another of the heads, while Sora charged forward and hammered the remaining head with his Keyblade.

As the beast winced slightly, Hercules escaped his sharp fangs and fell to his knees, gasping a little. But it wasn't long before he was back on his feet. He reared back mightily and slammed his fist into Cerberus's chest. The canine let out a pained roar.

"Stand back, you two," Cloud murmured.

"Huh?"

Sora and Hercules turned around, and they thought they saw Cloud's wing flap.

"This will put an end to it..."

Cloud suddenly leaped into the air and began a series of rapid slashes. The incredible attack was almost too fast for the eye to follow—Omnislash.

"Wow…," Sora murmured in awe.

Cerberus let loose a final howl toward the sky before his huge frame fell onto its side and disappeared in a flash.

"We did it!" Sora jumped with joy and landed with his arms around Cloud.

"Hmph. About time I found my way home," Cloud said wearily as he peeled the boy off of him.

Hercules let out a small chuckle as he watched them. "That should put the Coliseum back to normal," he said with a smile. "Let's go tell Phil the good news!"

As the three of them chattered away, filled with relief and happiness, a tall man appeared in a burst of smoke.

"Uh, 'scuse me, aren't you forgetting a few loose ends? Yeah, hi, I'm right here."

He sounded a little depressed, which made him even creepier than usual.

"Hades!"

The wicked Lord of the Dead was still around.

He eyed the shorter trio and bit his nails unhappily. "I finally find a trap with all the right trappings, and what do you do? You go and ruin it. Okay, the thing about deadly mazes? You're supposed to *die* in them. But I see this is going to take a more hands-on approach!"

Hades clenched his fists, gathering his strength, then thrust them skyward as the pale-blue flame of his hair blazed a bright red.

"Hey, uh, Herc, I think I know another trick to making it as a hero," Sora said with complete calm as he readied his Keyblade.

"Oh yeah?" Following Sora's lead, Hercules prepared himself for another fight.

"Let's hear it." Cloud did the same.

"At the end of the day…make sure you're still standing!"

The three of them didn't feel like they would be losing today.

"Oh, give me a break, pipsqueaks!" Hades summoned a large fire-ball and hurled it toward Sora and his companions.

"You won't beat us so easily!" Sora swatted the fireball back with his Keyblade, while Cloud rushed forward around it for an unavoidable blindside.

"Cheeky little snots, aren'tcha!"

"Hey, no hogging the spotlight, Cloud!"

Hercules flexed his arms, gearing up for his big attack, then slammed his fists into the ground with as much strength as he could muster. The impact sent a shock wave rumbling through the earth right toward Hades.

"Rrgh!" the Lord of the Dead yelped as he hurtled through the air.

"You had enough?"

"Don't think you've won yet! I've got over five hundred million lives! Sure, most of them are ones I took… But I will be back!" With that parting shot, Hades poofed away in retreat.

The air itself seemed to relax around them. Everything seemed brighter, too.

"The two of you are really something." Sora grinned at Hercules and Cloud.

"That's because we're heroes," Herc said with a smile.

"Heroes, huh…" Cloud whispered.

"Yeah. But hey, Phil must be worried. Ready to leave?" Hercules asked.

Sora gave a happy nod.

"Holy Hera! You guys made it back in one piece?!"

Phil greeted Sora and the others with a smile when they returned to the lobby.

"O ye of little faith," Sora replied proudly.

Hercules held out his right hand to Sora. "Thanks, Sora. I couldn't have done this without you."

Sora responded by clasping Herc's hand, but then he noticed something. "Hey, where's Cloud?" he asked, peering around.

"What, the schlimazel with the perky haircut? He left. Somethin'
about gettin' a jump on his next journey," Phil replied.

"What?! He could've at least said good-bye…" Sora let go of Herc's
hand and slumped in disappointment.

*What a jerk, just leaving like that. And right when we were getting
to be friends, too.*

"Ya know, he did leave a message. He said, 'Give my best to the
hero and the hero-to-be.'"

"Wait, hero-to-be? Me?" *Wow, Cloud thinks I'm a hero?!*

"In other words, kid, you're still in the junior leagues."

"Aww, man." Sora drooped sadly with both hands on his knees. *I
thought I did pretty good out there.*

"Ha-ha! I'm sure you'll make a great hero one day, Sora. I
could use a friend like you to help keep Olympus safe. Whaddaya say?" Hercules said, resting an encouraging hand on Sora's
shoulder.

"Tempting offer, but I have to go. Got friends waiting. But if ya
ever need me again, I'll come running!" Sora replied to Herc, smiling again. The hero's hand was big and warm. *Hope I can be a hero
like him someday.*

"Good to know. Give my best to your friends." Herc gave Sora a
hearty pat on the back.

"Will do."

"And kid, you keep at the hero biz. You got potential. Drop by if
you ever want some training!"

Finally, Phil gave Sora some stern words of advice.

"Thanks, Phil! Well, I'll see you guys later!"

Sora waved at the two of them, then dashed out of the lobby into
the courtyard.

Mickey, did that do it?

*   *   *

The monitor in the study showed Sora speaking to the sky from the courtyard. While Mickey and the others had only been able to watch with this world, Sora had been able to put everything back the way it should be with the help of his two friends, Hercules and Cloud.

"Yup, Sora…thank you," Mickey said to Sora on the screen.

Beside him, Donald cocked his head in confusion. "Hey, wait. This time we didn't get a video."

Every time Sora had restored the previous worlds, a video of events that Jiminy had no memory of recording had appeared on the monitor. This time there was nothing.

"Right. Those scenes—they originated in *my* mind," Riku replied.

"Huh?" Donald was confused.

"When you got rid of the bugs, you gave me deeper access to the memories associated with those worlds. The things I saw must have found their way back through the link and shown up on your monitor."

"Well, whaddaya know. If those memories came from deep within the journal itself, then it's really no wonder why they're unfamiliar. They don't belong to any of us!" Jiminy said, nodding several times.

So those videos were special memories, unknown even to the data itself. Still, he had never heard of a journal having a mind of its own. Riku said that he was data within the journal, but not the journal itself. The will of the journal and Data-Riku's existence seemed like separate things.

What was going on with the journal?

While Jiminy pondered all of this, Goofy spoke up. "Hmm? Something's happenin'…"

A strange newcomer had appeared before Sora on the monitor.

"Huh? No way!"

Recognizing who it was, Mickey jumped toward the screen.

Gah-ha-ha-ha! Long time no see!

* * *

The voice booming from the speakers was both familiar and unwelcome.

"Pete's here?! How'd you get in?" Mickey shouted.

Hearing his name, Pete looked up at the sky and spoke.

> *Same way as youse did. Thought I'd take a little vacay from the outside world.*

Somehow, Pete knew that Mickey and his friends were in the Datascape.

> *Well, this here world belongs to me, so mitts off!*

With that, Pete turned away from Sora and trotted off into a mysterious space swirling with an odd white light.

"He must be up to something. Quick! After him!" Mickey called.

Sora nodded and hurried through the portal after Pete.

CHAPTER 6
Agrabah

Little by little, the world is waking up. And it's changing, too. Every world can change, whether by healing or by hurting. I want to believe that sleep always ends in waking.

Beyond Pete's mysterious portal was a dusty city made of stone. Sora could feel the hot, dry air against his skin.

He searched the area nearby, but there was no sign of Pete.

It seemed like Mickey knew that Pete guy, but what could he be scheming?

Sora started walking, looking around as he went. Nothing jumped out at him as a potential hiding place, but he didn't get the sense that the guy would be easy to find.

Either way, the streets were really quiet. There were shops here and there, but not a soul to be found. Instead of the people who should have been living there, there were those same blocks from before. *Isn't there anybody I can ask?*

He set off in search of people, but as usual, Heartless barred the way. Someone must have hurt this world, too.

After scattering the Heartless before him, Sora found a plaza with a large gate. Beyond it was a great building with a round, richly colored roof. Maybe it was a palace or something? Standing in front of the gates was a young man who appeared to be thinking something over.

"Hey, there," Sora called. "How come everybody's indoors?"

The youth turned around in slight surprise. "Oh, you're human," he said, rubbing his chest. "Strange blocks? Weird monsters? Pick a reason. I managed to escape from that cave, but I've got to make sure my friend from the palace is safe, so— Hey, should you be out here? It's not safe on the streets," the young man said to Sora with concern. He seemed nice.

I don't think he's a bad guy. "I can take care of myself," Sora replied with a smile.

"Ha-ha, I stand corrected. Well, just keep both eyes open, okay?"

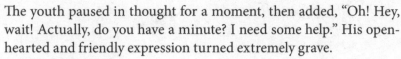

The youth paused in thought for a moment, then added, "Oh! Hey, wait! Actually, do you have a minute? I need some help." His open-hearted and friendly expression turned extremely grave.

"Sure, what's up?"

"I'm looking for a friend of mine. Her name's Jasmine, and she's... Well, she's special. I've been worried sick, but I can't seem to track her down. I'll keep checking around the palace. If it's all right—"

Sora replied before the young man could finish. "Say no more. I'm looking for somebody, too, so I'll keep an eye out for Jasmine while I search the city. It's no trouble!"

"Great! You're a lifesaver. I'm Aladdin, by the way."

A smile spread on Aladdin's face as he held out his right hand to Sora.

Sora clasped it firmly and introduced himself, too. "Sora! Nice to meet you. I'll let you know what I find, okay? Catch ya later!"

"Okay. Thanks, Sora!"

Sora gave a firm nod, then ran off in search of Jasmine and Pete.

Man, the streets were a tangled mess. The big avenue also served as a bazaar, but the stone homes on either side were clustered together to create an intricate maze.

Sora pushed onward, totally lost the entire time, until he heard a woman's voice. He stopped in the alleyway.

"...ry you? Not in a million years, you snake!"

Sora hurried toward it and found a girl arguing with a thin man behind some blocks. Both were richly dressed, but where the girl appeared to be honest and strong-willed, the man had an uncanny aura about him that could not be entirely concealed.

"Heh-heh-heh. You would do well to reconsider, my dear. I would so hate to see you hurt."

"My answer will never change, Jafar! I would rather die than marry you!"

"Rrgh! That can be arranged!" The man called Jafar held his staff aloft.

"Leave her alone!" Sora jumped between them and faced the man, keeping the girl safe behind him.

"Who are you?" she asked uncertainly.

He glanced back at her and asked, "The name's Sora. Umm... Are you Jasmine?"

She gave a small nod.

"Aladdin's been looking for you."

"What?! Aladdin!" Jafar reacted to the name, and his eyebrows shot up to make his mean-looking face even more unpleasant. "I thought I was rid of that useless street rat! Hmm... No matter. I can find him once I have dealt with you!"

Jafar swung his staff upward again.

"Jasmine, stay back. I'll get this weirdo out of your hair," Sora called out before charging toward Jafar. He swung his Keyblade up and struck the man on his bearded chin.

"Ungh!" A moment later, Jafar teleported away. So this guy could wield magic... As Sora was trying to figure out where he'd gone, a giant ball of fire descended from above.

"Look out!" Jasmine cried.

Thanks to her warning, Sora dodged it by a hairbreadth, then looked back along the path it had taken to find Jafar on a rooftop. Sora sprang from the ground, arced through the air to the top of the building, and slammed his Keyblade into his foe.

"How's *that*?"

"Grrrah! This is far from over!" Jafar spat. Staggering away, he vanished thanks to the same magic from before.

"Thank you, Sora." Jasmine came out of hiding and hurried up to him.

"No problem, but...how come that guy was bothering you?"

"Jafar? It's absolutely infuriating..."

Jasmine quietly began to explain her circumstances.

Right about then, Jafar was catching his breath in a corner of the bazaar.

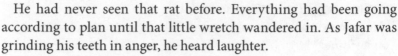

He had never seen that rat before. Everything had been going according to plan until that little wretch wandered in. As Jafar was grinding his teeth in anger, he heard laughter.

"Gah-ha-ha-ha! Rodent troubles?"

The one who appeared before Jafar was a tubby, mean-looking character with a large mouth and ears.

It was Pete, the same villain Sora was hunting.

"I've got your fix right here, pally."

"What? How dare you address me so—" Jafar narrowed his eyes at Pete's high-handed response—until he noticed what Pete was holding. "That lamp! It's the one I seek! The magic, wish-granting lamp!"

It was one of this world's legends.

Pete smirked. Jafar's reaction was exactly what he expected. "Not exactly. I used the glitches in this world to create a fax…facsimuh… A copy." He held out the lamp to Jafar.

"'Galichess'? Of what powerful sorcery do you speak? Give it to me at once!" Jafar practically snatched the lamp away from Pete.

"Pushy, pushy." Pete crossed his arms as Jafar stared intently at the lamp. "Just do ol' Pete a favor and plunge this world into darkn— Hmm?"

Jafar broke out in raucous laughter. "Heh-heh. HAAA-ha-ha-ha! At last, all of my plans will be realized!" He stroked the lamp and called, "Heed me, spirit of the lamp! For my first wish, I desire the power to stop anyone who gets in my way! Yes… Yes!"

A powerful light radiated from the lamp and enfolded Jafar's body.

"Wow, so you're a real princess? Who does Jafar think he is?"

Sora had been listening to Jasmine's story.

"Unfortunately, he's the royal vizier. And he's plotting something terrible, I know it. But when I tried to warn the others in the palace, no one would believe me. Jafar is a respected man." She lowered her gaze and shook her head sadly.

"Yeah, what's going on with the city?"

"I'm not sure. All these strange blocks appeared, and that was just the excuse Jafar needed to make his move. While everyone was distracted by the chaos, he tried to capture me." Jasmine let out a heavy, gloomy sigh.

Now that you mention it, Aladdin did say Jasmine was special... Sora asked Jasmine another question: "Does Aladdin know about Jafar?"

"No. Not yet. I wish I could talk to him..." Jasmine lifted her eyes, fighting back tears. "Wait, how do you know about Aladdin?!"

Sora stepped back a bit—Jasmine almost seemed ready to grab him.

"I ran into him in front of the palace," he answered. "He said he escaped from some cave..."

"He's alive! Oh, that's wonderful!" Jasmine clasped her hands in front of her chest, closing her eyes in relief and joy. Apparently, she had believed Aladdin was gone forever.

"Uh-huh. And he was worried sick about you. Let's go find him, and you can get the full story."

"Wonderful! I'll follow you."

Jasmine nodded enthusiastically with a brilliant smile.

As soon as she spotted Aladdin in the plaza, Jasmine ran past Sora and over to him.

"Jasmine! You're okay!"

"Aladdin! I'm glad you're all right."

A short distance away, Sora watched the two of them gazing into each other's eyes and felt a bit of relief. Now all that needed to be done was to find Pete.

"I just wish the same could be said for Agrabah." Jasmine's expression clouded over.

"Don't worry, I've got the answer to our problems right here. See, I was in this weird cave in the desert, and wait'll you see what I found. Jafar's days are numbered!"

As Aladdin finished talking, a looming black shadow fell over them.

"We shall see about that, street rat!"

It was the vizier.

"Jafar!"

Sora ran over to Aladdin and Jasmine, summoning his Keyblade. But before he could stop him, Jafar seized Jasmine by the arm.

"Nnnh! Let me...go!"

"Jasmine!" Aladdin cried, running over to grab Jafar, but some strange force knocked him away.

"Heh-heh-heh! Now all of Agrabah belongs to me. With the princess for my wife, I shall rule this land as sultan!"

"No way..." Sora tried to take Jasmine back himself, only to be blasted back by the same mysterious power.

"Hm-hm! Yes way! You see, the lamp has given me a most remarkable power. No one can defy me now."

"Lamp?! But how did you—?" Back on his feet, Aladdin reached into his pocket.

"Sadly, weddings do take time to plan. And since *I'm* the one speaking now, you wretches can forever hold your peace!" Jafar held the lamp aloft.

"Wha—?!"

Sora briefly closed his eyes against a sudden wave of bright light.

When he reopened them—everything looked the same, except that Jasmine and Jafar were no longer there.

"No! They're gone! Quick, Aladdin, we have to go after them!"

Sora called out to Aladdin, ready to get going, but there was something off about him. He was completely still. In his hand was a lamp that looked a lot like the one Jafar had earlier.

"Um... Aladdin?"

Sora waved a hand in front of the young man's open, unblinking eyes, but he didn't even twitch. It was as if time had been stopped for him.

> *Jafar has hit the city with some kind of powerful spell.*

Confused, Sora heard Mickey's voice. "Mickey! You seeing this? What's the diagnosis?"

> *Well, uh… Gosh. It looks like… It looks like Jafar has managed to stop time for the entire city!*

"Huh? But I can still move," Sora replied, looking at himself.

> *You have the Keyblade. Jafar didn't account for that. Still, even the Keyblade won't hold the spell at bay forever.*

"What?! Then I need to get out of here! But…I can't just leave Aladdin and the city like this."

As Sora talked to Mickey, a parrot was observing him. The spell had no effect on him, meaning he had to be in cahoots with Jafar. With a flap of his brightly colored wings, he snatched up the lamp from Aladdin's hand.

"H-hey!" Sora shouted

With the lamp firmly in both feet, the parrot—Iago—flew off. "What?" he yelled. "Ain't ya ever heard of the three-talon discount? Jafar wouldn't tell me what this lamp does, but whatever it is, it's gonna make me one happy parrot!"

Iago then fluttered off.

"Ugh, great!"

> *Sora, you've got to get that lamp back! There's a friend inside who can help you!*

*   *   *

Mickey sounded a bit panicked, too.

"'Inside'? Well, if you say so!"

> *Remember, you don't have much time. You need to find the lamp before it's too late!*

"I'm on it."

Sora took off running, but he had no idea where Iago had gone.

Well, at least there was a silver lining to all this—the time spell had frozen the Heartless, too.

Sora's first stop was the royal palace, but there was no sign of Iago. "Where could he be…?"

He was getting winded after all this running around, but he had to hurry if he didn't want to end up frozen, too.

Now that he thought about it—that alley where he found Jasmine and Jafar the first time would be a great hiding spot. With a new destination in mind, Sora dashed through the streets.

"There he is! Please, you have to give that back!"

"Oh, I'm sorry. I had no idea it meant so much to you! Now I *know* it's worth hangin' on to! Buh-bye!"

Iago flew off again. Sora got the feeling he was going to have to take the lamp back by force. He ran after the parrot, back through the bazaar and toward the palace gates.

Spying Iago atop the roof of a certain shop, Sora paused to catch his breath. *Okay, no asking nicely this time. I've gotta get the jump on him!*

Observing his quarry from cover, Sora pounced the moment Iago landed.

"Gotcha!" Sora caught hold of Iago with both hands and glared at the bird.

"Eep! I plead insanity! I'm beggin' ya, cut a bird some slack!" The parrot let go of the lamp and desperately pleaded for mercy. Sora *was* pretty intense; Iago was probably bracing for the worst.

"I'll let you off the hook this time. But there won't be any second chances."

"Eeek!"

The moment Sora released Iago, he screeched in a very un-parrot-like manner and fluttered away. Sora scooped up the lamp from where it had fallen on the ground and peered at it closely.

"Whew! About time."

The dully gleaming antique looked ancient. Why had Aladdin possessed it in the first place? This was what he found in the cave, right?

Sora leaned in closer to see if there was something else about the lamp he was missing, and it suddenly wiggled.

"Wh-what?!"

The lamp jumped again, then spat out a jet of smoke.

"Whoa!"

What emerged from the lamp was…

"Troubles, Al? Whoa! …Hey, wait. You're not Al."

A large blue man was floating in the air above Sora. Upon closer inspection, Sora saw that his form didn't have legs. Instead of standing on two feet, he was hovering.

He couldn't sit here being shocked, though. Time was of the essence.

Maybe "Al" is Aladdin! Let's see.

"Yeah, Aladdin can't move 'cause Jafar stopped time. Um…who are you?" Sora asked.

The blue figure spun a circle in the air and snapped his fingers. "The name's Genie, last name 'of the lamp.' Hey, how ya doin'? Ya got, like, issues, man? Just make a wish! Problems solved! Wrongs righted! Service while you wait!" he rambled.

Sora blinked. "You'll grant all my wishes?" he asked.

Genie leaned in close, maybe too close, and held up three fingers. "No sirree. Three per customer, while supplies last. That's the limit. Can't expect other people to take care of every little thing."

Sora fell into thought for a moment, partially overwhelmed by Genie's enthusiasm and partially because he couldn't quite believe that *any* wish could be granted.

"Maybe you don't believe me?" Genie inquired uncomfortably.

Is that even possible, to have whatever you wish come true? It sounds like something out of a dream. Well, Genie doesn't seem like a bad guy; plus, he's friends with Aladdin. I can probably go along with him.

"Hmm, then I better make my wishes count. I'll tell you one thing—I wish this world had fewer problems!"

"You wished it, kiddo, you got it. Badda-bing!" Genie twirled in the air with a snap and a wink. The world rumbled slightly.

"Well? Whaddaya think of your new, totally phantom-free city?"

"Oh! Uh… They're gone! Thanks! So that unfroze time for Aladdin, too, right?"

"Huh? Oh dear." Genie shook his head. "Cue remorseful genie in three, two, one…"

"What?! You mean you didn't help him?" Sora's head drooped dejectedly.

"Well, you did say 'fewer problems'…Sorry, kid, I guess I just sorta went by the book."

Genie looked deflated as well. His dramatic show of disappointment actually helped Sora feel a bit better.

"No, it's my fault. I should've been more specific."

"Well, I won't have a half-granted wish on my permanent record! We'll call that one a freebie. And guess what—to make it up to you, I've even got a trace on your bad guy. How's that for service?" Genie put his arm around Sora's shoulder.

"Bad guy… You mean Jafar? Now we're talking! Let's try this again. Genie, I wish for you to take me to Jafar!"

"You got it, boss! Buckle up, 'cause here…we…gooo!" Genie extended his arms and began to spin, creating a whirlwind.

The tornado sent Sora and Genie flying all the way to a great statue of a tiger's head in the desert. There was something special about this place.

The tiger's mouth was shut—and standing before the statue was Jafar.
"Jafar!"

"What?! How did you get here? Ah, of course. So you have obtained the real lamp. And that preposterous weapon is also no doubt to blame." Jafar explained his theory, rubbing his chin confidently.

"What did you do with Jasmine?"

"My future queen is resting, on the far side of that door."

"Door? What door?" Sora replied.

The vizier sneered. "What door indeed? You will never find it, boy."

"You'll tell me once I'm done with you!"

"Oh-ho, I think not. Sadly, I must go steal Jasmine's heart. And you will not interfere again. Spirit of the lamp! Heed my second wish! Keep these pests from following me!"

Jafar swung his hand upward, and an odious mist engulfed the area.

"What are you—?"

Sora observed his surroundings cautiously for a moment, but nothing happened. The fog eventually cleared, too, but it had given Jafar enough time to vanish.

"...Everything looks hunky-dory here, kid," Genie said, flitting back and forth.

"Sheesh. Where did Jafar run off to now?"

"Well, normally the tiger's mouth is open...," Genie commented with his head to one side.

"It is?! That must mean... There it is!"

Sora found a familiar fissure in the air next to the tiger's head.

"What's this?"

"Wait here, Genie!"

Sora plunged into the System Sector.

"Genie never changes, does he?" Goofy commented happily, watching the events on the monitor.

"I'd like to see Aladdin and Jasmine again, too."

Donald smiled a little as he remembered. The world on the screen was built from the records of their journey, so it was only natural that the two of them would get sentimental. Seeing the worlds visited and the friends they met with Sora made them want to set off on another adventure.

"Where did Pete go, though?" Mickey cocked his head to the side.

"He sure doesn't seem to be from the datascape." Jiminy crossed his arms and thought.

"My guess is, Pete found a way to get into the journal," Riku replied to the two of them.

"You mean there's another way to get into this world besides the computer in the real world?"

"That's impossible. The only copy of the journal is here." Mickey quickly shot down Jiminy's suggestion. They weren't going to get any answers about what was happening with the journal and datascape without Sora's aid.

"I'm sure Sora will get it all sorted out," Donald replied. Whether in the datascape or in the real world, Sora was always Sora, and he had absolute faith.

"Pete worries me, though. We have to be prepared for the worst with him," Mickey replied, then looked up at the boy swinging his Keyblade inside the monitor.

"If we need to be prepared for the worst…there may be something we can do," Riku said softly.

Mickey and the others turned toward him expectantly.

After Sora left the System Sector, the mouth of the tiger yawned open. Genie peeked inside it, then wrapped his arms around himself and shivered.

"Hmm, this isn't going to be easy, chief. I'm picking up a triple dose of traps on my lamp-dar."

"It's that stupid lamp Jafar's got. But if he's cranking up the security, that can only mean Jasmine's inside," Sora replied, peeking into the tiger's mouth like Genie. Adding more traps was all but announcing that a valuable treasure lay beyond them.

"Smells like a theory to me."

"Let's go find her and put Jafar in his place."

Sora stepped into the tiger's maw. The Cave of Wonders within it was dusty and dim. The occasional torch along the walls cast some light, but it wasn't really enough to illuminate the way forward.

After traveling an unpleasantly narrow path that was rotten with Heartless, they heard an ominous rumbling.

"What? Whoa!"

Realizing what was causing the noise, Sora stopped just in the nick of time. It was a trap that sent huge, round boulders tumbling toward him. If one of those rolled over him, he wouldn't stand a chance.

Once he'd figured out the timing so as not to get flattened, Sora sprinted down the narrow path in one shot.

"Phew…"

He paused for a breather as he spotted the exit to the next chamber. Genie suddenly appeared behind him. "Hmm, this place smells fishy, and we're a long way from water."

"Jafar must be close, then. You think there's hope for Aladdin and the city?" Sora asked, looking up at his bobbing blue companion.

"Well, sure there is! A few swift kicks in Jafar's caboose oughtta kick-start time for Agrabah. And Al will be free as a bird! I'm jealous, really. I'd give anything for that freedom, but I'm stuck until my master wishes me free," he said with a sad shake of his head.

"You want to be free… Sorry. I never put myself in your shoes."

He's been trapped inside a lamp for so long—must be lonely, not to mention painful.

"That's okay, I don't have any. But there's genie-hood for you! Phenomenal, cosmic power… Itty-bitty living space… Wow, déjà vu! I think I said the same thing to Al. Ya know, he seemed to understand more than the others..." Genie's eyes closed slightly as he recalled that time.

"This cave is where you two met, right? Aladdin's a good friend. When we first met, he was looking out for me, too. Come on, Genie. He needs us."

"Lead the way!" Genie grinned at Sora's words of encouragement, whirled in the air, and returned to the lamp.

"Time to get moving!"

They finally reached the main chamber—the great cavernous room where Genie's magic lamp had once rested. Jafar was standing on top of a raised platform that looked somewhat like an altar.

I'm going to defeat him no matter what! I'll save Jasmine and Aladdin!

"It's over, Jafar! You've got no place else to run!" Sora thrust his Keyblade at his enemy.

"What? How could you have eluded all those traps? Hmph, it seems clear to me now... You are no street rat. Why not serve me? Whatever you desire, I can make it happen," Jafar purred.

"Whatever I desire, huh? All right..." Sora smirked. "I desire for Aladdin to be sultan. Make that happen!"

"Him?! Do not toy with me. Perhaps you need a lesson in what a true ruler can do. That is, *if* you can tell the true ruler from the others!" Jafar abruptly split into three copies. Each one wore his arrogant expression, poised to strike.

But without a moment's hesitation, Sora approached one of the viziers and whacked it with his Keyblade.

"Gah! How could you tell?!"

"Because the others are see-through! Give up, Jafar! Let Jasmine go! The city, too!" Sora was getting annoyed as he jabbed his Keyblade at Jafar.

"Rrgh! You leave me little choice! I was saving my final wish to make Jasmine love me..." Jafar snarled, then swung his staff upward. "...but now I will simply have to take the princess and city by force! Spirit of the lamp! I wish for you to make me an all-powerful genie!"

The vizier seemed much more formidable now. Upon making his wish, he was swallowed into a great light.

"Where'd he go?"

Jafar had vanished without a trace.

"Haaa-ha-ha-haaa! I told you, boy: You will never find the far side of the door. And now...such power! Nothing can stop me from shaping the world as I see fit! Savor your final moments, boy. Soon, I will crush you!"

The very cave itself was letting out a continuous rumble. At this rate, the world would become Jafar's plaything. *I have to do something. But I don't know where to go... What can I do?*

Don't panic, Sora. Jafar's closer than you think.

He could hear a calm voice from the air. His heart filled with relief, Sora smiled and called back, "Mickey! Are you sure?"

Right, I'm not alone in this. Mickey and Genie are with me.

Think about it—what do we know about hidden doors? Jafar must be inside the Keyhole! You've got to find it, and quickly.

"Leave it to me," Sora replied, surveying the chamber. Well, one place jumped out at him. Those red-and-black blocks didn't belong here, and there was something behind them.

Sora struck the blocks with his Keyblade, and they vanished as they always did.

Behind them, a Keyhole appeared.

"Here goes!"

Sora held his Keyblade up to the Keyhole and stepped into the realm beyond the door.

It was scorching hot and filled with bubbling lava. Jafar was hardly recognizable now, transformed into an enormous crimson genie. But his hateful glare was still the same.

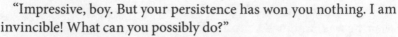

"Impressive, boy. But your persistence has won you nothing. I am invincible! What can you possibly do?"

Genie Jafar hurled a colossal ball of magma Sora's way. The boy barely managed to dodge in time. "Rrgh…," he muttered. "I'll get back to you on that…"

The heat was making it hard to breathe.

Genie here. Do you read me, Sora?

"Loud and clear, Genie!"

This time, the voice from the air was Genie's, cheerful and energetic as ever despite the dire circumstances.

He's not kidding about the invincible part. None of your attacks can hurt him. But Jafar is a genie now. Which means…

As Sora calmed down and started looking around, he spotted that parrot—Iago—circling overhead with a lamp held tightly in his talons.

"The lamp! Roger that, Genie! Over and out!" Sora replied briefly to Genie, then pursued Iago by hopping on the scattered blocks.

"You've scurried around long enough. This is the end, boy!"

Genie Jafar fired a beam from his eyes with the power to slow Sora down. He narrowly evaded it, but Iago took that opportunity to fly farther away.

"Huff…huff… Hoo! I'm gettin' all flapped out."

But the parrot was starting to get tired. Of course he was; that lamp was a heavy burden for a bird playing keep-away.

Sora used the chance to dash atop the blocks and smack the lamp out of Iago's talons with his Keyblade.

"Eep! Okay, okay, I give up! Just watch the tail feathers!" Iago flapped his wings loudly and made his escape, but Sora ignored him and went after the fallen lamp instead.

"No! My lamp!"

Genie Jafar extended his arms in his first display of panic, but Sora was one step ahead of him. As he scooped up the lamp, Genie had one last bit of advice:

Now, Sora! Trap Jafar in the lamp!

Without a moment wasted, Sora held the lamp aloft and cried out, "Right! Time for you to see your new home, Jafar!"

The lamp glimmered for a moment, and then Jafar was sucked into the opening with terrific force. Once the vizier had disappeared, the lamp let out a feeble rattling protest in Sora's hands. The sound gradually faded, and the lamp eventually vanished.

"Is it...over?" Sora panted, exhausted after his grueling game of tag.

Unfortunately, it wasn't. Pete had been watching from somewhere, and he finally came tromping out. "Grrrrr! No fair! That clown was supposed to cast this world into darkness!" he grumbled loudly to himself.

"Huh? Pete!"

This was the last place he'd expected to find him, but Sora had stumbled across the one he was looking for. He made to chase after Pete straightaway, only for Genie to pop in beside him and bring him to a halt.

"Sora! Leaving already?"

"Yeah, Genie... I've gotta go. Will you help Jasmine back to town and give the lamp to Aladdin?" Sora paused, looking at Genie with a hint of melancholy.

"Consider it done! That's wish number two!"

So that counted as a wish—which meant there was one more left.

"So what's on the menu for *número tres*, amigo?" Genie asked expectantly.

I already know my third wish, but I shouldn't be the one to make it.

"I give my third wish to Aladdin."

Genie's eyes went wide.

"He found the lamp first... Well, what matters is, he was your friend first. He'll do what's right."

"Gosh, Sora..."

Genie hid his face with an arm as if there were tears in his eyes—or so Sora thought until he spun merrily through the air, just like when they first met.

"That was beautiful! I'll tell Al that's how ya feel. Thanks!"

"Are you kidding? Thank *you*! Take care, Genie. Tell everybody I said 'hi.'"

And with that, Sora hurried after Pete. He shouldn't be too far ahead yet.

After dashing through the cave, he leaped out of the tiger's mouth.

However, Pete was waiting for him.

"All right, Pete! You're through running."

When Sora readied his Keyblade, Pete merely smirked. "Heh-heh-heh, who said anything about running?"

He seems really sure of himself. What's going on here?

"All right, come on out and show him who's boss...Maleficent," Pete called, and a woman robed in black appeared—Maleficent.

"Who are you?"

"An amusing jest, boy, but one I will not abide. If you desire a reminder of my power...then I shall give you one!" The evil fairy quickly raised the staff in her hand, creating a shot of green flame that struck Sora.

"Agh!"

Sora's Keyblade fell from his grasp and stuck into the ground.

"Isn't that odd?" Maleficent murmured, and the Keyblade floated into the air. Sora tried to jump up and retrieve it, but he was too late. The fairy swiftly swung her staff and easily shattered the Keyblade right in front of his eyes.

"...What?!" Sora could only watch in shock.

With a sidelong glance at him, Maleficent let out a cackle. "So we see, 'twas but a lie. And now that it's gone, this world shall be mine to rule."

What should I do? I can't fight without my Keyblade. But I have to try.

"Yes, my loyal minions. Drag all that you see into deepest darkness!"

As Sora tried to stand, Maleficent summoned a horde of Heartless in front of him. The monsters slowly encircled and trapped him.

"Agh…!"

At this rate, the darkness would overtake him. Sora braced himself, but just as the Heartless descended upon him, they were wiped out in a flash.

"You okay?" someone called to him.

He raised his head to see Riku and Mickey had arrived. The two of them looked back at Sora with those same familiar smiles.

"Maleficent. What are you doing here in the datascape?" asked Mickey, glaring at her.

"'Date escape'? Spare me your dull details," she replied with a scowl.

"But since you're wonderin', it was all my idea, you bozo," Pete boasted to Mickey. "We caught wind right away you was up to somethin', see. So, I decided to pay ya a little visit on Maleficent's orders. I was just takin' a peek into your room, and that's how yours truly got sucked into the light show. I woke up all by my lonesome in the weirdest place. Then I did some diggin' around. Turns out this place connects right to that there castle o' yours," Pete explained in a rush. Then he snorted and crossed his arms. "Or at least it *did*, before I took control of the only way out," he added with a sneer.

Sora finally rose to his feet and got into a fighting stance. "So you're the one who cut the link!"

Maleficent replied in Pete's stead. "Rest assured, both worlds shall be mine before long. Once I have immersed this one in darkness, I can send my Heartless horde back into your castle!"

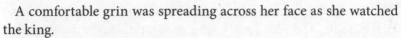

A comfortable grin was spreading across her face as she watched the king.

"No!" Mickey cried in shock.

Maleficent continued slowly, "The long slumber has ended, and a new era has begun—one where all worlds belong to me! But my worlds must be free of light, and yours shine far too brightly. This time, it is you who will sleep!" She waved her hand tauntingly.

"Wrong. This is one world I won't let you touch!"

Riku sprang toward her. But...

"Hmph! Foolish boy!"

A burst of green flame from her staff hit Riku hard, and he screamed.

"Arrrgh!"

When the boy lost consciousness, Pete picked him up from the ground.

"Riku!"

Mickey called his name, but he didn't move.

"Now, you, boy... You belong to the darkness, not the light. I shall take this one with me. I'm sure he will prove...useful." Maleficent vanished with a haughty laugh.

"Check aaaand mate! So long, suckers! Gah-ha-ha-ha!"

Pete let out a roar of laughter and disappeared after her—with Riku in tow.

"No!"

Sora tried to pursue them, but they were already gone.

"Riku..." Mickey lowered his head mournfully.

CHAPTER 7
Hollow Bastion

There are no coincidences; fate happens as it was planned. As for whose plan it is…I couldn't tell you. Not yet. But, Sora, we are friends. We will always be friends—always. Everyone you've met along the way—Riku, Mickey, Donald, and Goofy—we're all here for you. Don't forget that.

Riku's gone. Pete and Maleficent took him away, and it's all my fault, because I was careless.

After Sora had returned to the study in Disney Castle with Mickey, he wandered away to brood alone in the corner.

"This is terrible! Poor Riku."

Jiminy cradled his head after Mickey brought him up to speed.

"Say, fellas, hasn't Riku got all the journal data inside him?" Goofy was thinking with his arms crossed.

"If Maleficent casts him into the darkness…then the whole datascape will go kaplooie." Donald's face was tense with concern. Riku's abduction meant Maleficent had the data itself in her clutches. While they still didn't know what significance the lost memories held, it was easy to see how they might be used for evil.

"How many worlds still have bugs, Jiminy?" Mickey asked.

The cricket climbed atop the computer's keyboard and pressed several keys with his feet. "Err…just one, it looks like. We were so close, but now…" Jiminy shook his head. They really were almost done. But now, Riku was gone.

"That was your way home, huh…?" Sora murmured faintly. "Guys, I'm so sorry. I really blew it."

None of this would have happened if I were stronger. It didn't matter to Sora that this Riku was a vessel for data. Riku was Riku—his best friend.

"It's not your fault, Sora. And don't you worry. I'll take care of this." Mickey smiled and summoned his Keyblade into his hand.

"Y-yo-your Majesty?!" Jiminy sprang into the air.

"Well, why not? I'll find another way to fix the bugs, and rescue Riku, too!" the king declared before Sora and the others.

"Let me help, Mickey. This time, I won't let anyone take the Key…" Sora tried to call his Keyblade into his hand, but it didn't appear.

"Huh? That's weird. The Keyblade's not… I can't summon it!"

True, Maleficent had broken the Keyblade, but it had never failed him when he willed it to come. Now that it was broken, did that mean it would never come again?

"Sora…I'm sorry. Maleficent destroyed your Keyblade," Mickey told him sadly.

"For good?"

"I have to be honest with you. That Keyblade was something we wrote into the datascape from the outside. Now that we're trapped *inside* the datascape, there's no way for us to get it back."

"But I want to—"

Sora lowered his gaze. *I really…really hate this. I can't do anything.*

"I know. But you've already done a lot for us! It's time for me to see what I can do," Mickey said emphatically. "Now, you all sit tight right here!"

With those words of farewell, Mickey opened the door and set off with a resolute stride.

"I'm worried. Do you think the king needs help?" Donald watched him go with a hint of concern.

"Aw, he'll manage. You don't get to be king for nothin'!" Goofy replied.

Donald crossed his arms, clearly thinking hard about something. "Well, he can show those Heartless a thing or two, but…"

As the others talked, Sora stood still, lost in thought.

"Now Maleficent and Pete are on the loose. And let's not forget…" Jiminy deflated with a great sigh.

"The bugs… Gawrsh, this worryin' thing is contagious."

"But he definitely said to sit tight."

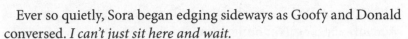

Ever so quietly, Sora began edging sideways as Goofy and Donald conversed. *I can't just sit here and wait.*

"Sora, what do you think we should do?" Donald asked, but there was no sign of the boy.

"...Um, Sora?" Donald ran all over the study. Sora wasn't there, not even under the desk or behind the bookshelves.

"He was there a second ago." Jiminy gave another sigh. Now they had one more problem to worry about.

"Uh, fellas, you don't think...?"

Goofy turned toward the door of the study.

Sora arrived at the final world where bugs remained, Hollow Bastion, and took in the sights and sounds of the mysterious machinery that surrounded him.

Even if I don't have a Keyblade, I can still help. I have to save Riku, at least.

A familiar form cut across Sora's path up ahead.

"Pete!" he shouted, running up to him.

"Hmm? You again? What's a has-been like you doin' here?" he scoffed rudely, all but saying that without his Keyblade Sora was no threat to him at all.

"Start talking, Pete! Where are you keeping Riku?"

"Well, shucks, if you wanna find out that bad, you're gonna have to catch me—*ya nitwit*! And good luck tryin'! I just finished riggin' the joint, Pete-style. You won't last ten steps!"

Pete sneered and dashed off.

"H-hey! That's what you think!"

"So long, sucker!"

Pete disappeared through a door into a great castle, and Sora ran after him in hot pursuit.

Inside, there was a large hall with two staircases going up either side.

"C'mon out, Pete!" Sora shouted, only for red-and-black blocks to suddenly appear surrounding him.

"Hey! Pete must want to trap me in."

"Gah-ha-ha-ha! You're a real piece of work, waltzin' in here when you can't do nothin'!" Pete bellowed with laughter atop the blocks.

"I can do enough to wipe that smug look off your face!"

"Oh, I'm shakin' in my boots. Heartless? Get 'im!"

At Pete's command, the Heartless arrived. *What do I do? I can't fight them without my Keyblade.*

"Now you all play nice while I finish settin' up our little puppet show."

"Get back here!" Sora shouted, but Pete hopped down from the blocks and out of sight. All that remained was Sora and a lot of Heartless. The monsters were getting closer and closer.

A single Heartless leaped at Sora and clawed him on the cheek.

"Ow!"

These guys would be nothing if I only had my Keyblade...!

Just then, Sora heard a familiar drawl and heavy footsteps. "Look out, Sora! Waa-ha-hoo-hooey!" Shield in hand, Goofy whirled into the blocks and sent them flying.

"Goofy!"

The captain of the guard stood protectively between Sora and the Heartless, then charged into the throng and dispersed them. He looked back at Sora with a grin. "Gawrsh, Sora! The king said to stay put. You shouldn'ta run off on your own like that."

Sora could tell Goofy was a little exasperated, and he did feel bad. He had ignored the king's concern, run off on his own, and then gotten himself trapped. If it weren't for Goofy's arrival, there was no telling what could have happened.

"I know, I'm sorry, I just—"

All I can do is stay put in the study and let the king handle it. I don't have my Keyblade anymore.

"Nope. Not another word. Let's get goin'."

"All right…I'm going." Sora obediently started trudging off toward the exit.

"A-hyuck, goin' where? It's this direction!" Goofy called from behind him, sounding puzzled.

"Huh? We aren't going back?" Sora asked. He turned around. *I mean, I can't fight anymore…*

"We're chasin' after Pete, aren't we? We gotta hurry, before he gets too far!"

"You're not mad? Thanks, Goofy, I owe ya."

Goofy looked so confused that Sora started getting confused, too. And then the captain laughed.

"Owe me for what? Ya said it yourself, Sora: Friends don't keep score."

"Right!"

Sora grinned and ran over to Goofy. He could barely resist the urge to hug him.

My Keyblade isn't all I have to fight with. I still have my friends.

"You didn't happen to see Donald, did ya?" Goofy asked Sora as they started walking.

"Huh? Donald's here, too?"

"We were lookin' for ya together but musta got split up somewhere along the way," Goofy said worriedly.

"I hope he's okay. We'll have to keep an eye out while we look for Pete."

"I wonder where he could've gone…?"

Sora and Goofy started their search by climbing the stairs to the second floor from the hall.

"Pete went through there, right?"

"I think so."

Sora couldn't be sure because he hadn't been able to see around the block wall. Still, he knew something suspicious lay ahead.

At the top of the stairs, Sora and Goofy found a big door directly across from the entrance.

"Doesn't seem to…nnngh…wanna open…" Goofy tilted his head in curiosity as he banged on the door.

Sora also gave it a close look. There were strange indentations carved into its surface. "Wait, check out these slots on the door. This shape must be the Heartless' emblem," he murmured. It was shaped like the mark on the Heartless.

"You're right! That is odd."

"If we find the pieces that fit in the slot…"

"I'm sure you're right, Sora. Let's track down the pieces that go in the emblem!"

Sora nodded at Goofy's idea. "I wonder where they could be, though…?"

"We'll just have to poke around."

As they walked away from the door, still talking…

"A-hyuck!"

"Donald!"

…they spotted a familiar white bottom and blue outfit exiting the castle.

Sora and Goofy dashed down the stairs and outside after their friend, but Donald was nowhere to be found.

"There he is!"

"Where?"

Goofy pointed out a passage lined with several blocks. Sora couldn't see Donald, though—he was probably already gone.

"Let's hurry!"

They dashed off again, only for Heartless and moving blocks to get in their way.

"Stay behind me, Sora!"

"Sorry, Goofy."

Sora made his way forward with Goofy and his shield protecting him. Not being able to use his Keyblade was really getting on his nerves.

After making their way through the path littered with blocks, they found a gondola that resembled a large cage. It appeared to lead underground.

"Guess we're supposed to ride it…?"

"Looks that way."

Sora and Goofy got on board, and the gondola descended. They arrived at a dim subterranean passageway.

"Where did Donald go?"

"I get the feeling he's around here."

In front of them was a fence that resembled the iron bars of a cell. It didn't look easy to get around.

"Isn't that him?" Goofy asked.

Sora could make out Donald's silhouette beyond the bars.

"Donald!"

He turned around at Sora's shout.

"We finally caught up." Goofy smiled, and Donald hurried over to the fence.

"Sora! And Goofy! Where did you wander off to? This is no time to go missing!" Donald said while poking his face through the bars.

"Aren't you the one who went missing?" Sora tried to protest, but Donald only scolded him further.

"Oh, whatever! Do you have any idea how worried I was?"

Still, it was no surprise that Donald was worried about Sora when he didn't have his Keyblade.

"Sorry, Donald. I dragged you guys into a real mess, and I hardly even know you."

Donald and Goofy shared a glance when Sora apologized.

Then, Donald erupted into laughter. "Now just wait a second! It was no trouble at all," he said, looking up at Sora.

"Huh?"

He wasn't sure what would motivate Donald to say such a thing.

"We kinda like gettin' dragged into your messes!" Goofy laughed.

"Um…why?"

"It's no fun watching from the other side of a computer screen!

We've been looking for an excuse to help—so we can go on adventures together, just like old times."

They wanted to have adventures together... It made Sora happy. He had always been on his own, but really he'd had everyone watching over him the whole time. Now, he wouldn't be alone at all.

"We may not be a new Keyblade, but you sure can count on us!" Goofy patted Sora on the shoulder.

"I don't know what to say. But I'll start with 'thanks'!" Sora said, blushing.

Donald waved his staff and said, "You just leave the Heartless to me. I'll show 'em who's boss! Now, how do I get out of here?"

Now that he mentioned it, that iron fence was still between them and Donald.

"How did you get in there?" Goofy asked.

"I used my magic on some Heartless, and then the bars came down," Donald replied. "Like this!"

Donald flourished his staff, and a fireball shot out of the tip. As he did, the lamp-like object next to him blazed to life, and the fence keeping the three apart rose upward.

"Whaddaya know! This thing responded to your magic."

"It did? Er, it did! Just like I...planned?"

Sora and Goofy cracked up as Donald sputtered unconvincingly. Though it was Sora's first time spending this long with the two of them, for some reason it felt like they'd been friends for a long time.

"By the way, I found this inside." Donald showed Sora a few peculiar, sparkling shards.

"You think they're..."

"...pieces of the emblem?"

Sora and Goofy looked at each other.

"Wak? What do you mean?" Donald cocked his head.

"Let's get back to the door!"

"Huh?"

Leaving Donald still confused, Sora and Goofy ran for the gondola.

"W-wait for me!"

"Better keep up if you don't want us to leave you, Donald!"

"Cut it out, Sora!"

Donald hustled after Sora and Goofy, waving his staff around.

With all three of them aboard, the gondola rose aboveground. They returned to the castle along the same path as before. Once he was inside, Sora looked back at Donald and Goofy and called, "Hurry it up! Last one to the door's a rotten egg!"

"Huh?"

"Wak! No fair! You didn't say anything about a race!"

Sora sprinted up the stairs to the door, two at a time, and turned around breathlessly. "First!"

"Gawrsh, Sora…Ya can't go runnin' off like that…" Goofy was catching his breath with a hand against the wall.

"No more sudden races!" Donald sat leaning against the wall with his feet splayed out.

"Are you sure you two aren't out of shape?"

"Of course not!" Donald shot to his feet and protested.

"Let's hurry up and try the pieces, Sora. Hopefully it does the trick with the door."

Goofy moved away from the wall as well, then stood before the door and hurried Sora along.

Sora took the pieces Donald had found and tried placing them in the indentation on the door. It was a perfect fit. The fragments let out a dazzling light, and the door opened.

"It worked!"

"You said Pete went through here, right?" Donald peeked uneasily through the crack of the door. They could feel a breeze whistling through. The door must be an exit to the outside.

"Yeah… Something about a 'puppet show'…," Sora muttered

nervously. *What did he mean, "puppet show"? And why does that have me so worried?*

"Whatever's in there, fellas, we'd better watch out," Goofy advised.

Sora nodded, then looked at what lay ahead. He was afraid; anyone would be. *But we have to keep moving and save Riku!*

"Pete's the one that's gonna have to watch out!"

Sora stepped through the door, with Donald and Goofy close behind. After a moment, the floor suddenly began to rise. By the time they realized what was going on, it was already moving pretty fast, and they finally figured out that they were riding on a gigantic gondola.

"Wow! Where do ya think it leads?" Goofy wondered idly, gazing up at the sky.

"Look out!" Donald pushed Sora out of the way as Heartless suddenly descended from the air. The winged monsters were trying to get at Sora.

"Stay back, Sora!" Donald leaped and cast a powerful Thunder spell on the Heartless.

"Here I go!"

Goofy followed it up by whirling into the Heartless at high speed, scattering them for good.

They were coming after me, and all I can do is escape. It was hard, but Sora did his best to at least keep moving and not get in the others' way.

Once they had managed to defeat all the Heartless, Donald and Goofy sat down on the spot, looking a bit worse for the wear.

I shouldn't have made them race me earlier.

"I'm sorry I couldn't do more to help…"

"That doesn't sound like you at all!" Donald stood up and tapped Sora in the chest with his staff. "This isn't the first time you've lost your Keyblade, right?"

"Huh?"

When Sora reacted with surprise, Donald just waved his staff harder.

"That didn't happen to this Sora," Goofy reminded him.

"I forgot!" Donald finally put two and two together, then got ahold of himself and looked up at Sora. "But you're still you!" His face was completely serious.

Filled with happiness, Sora grinned. "Donald, Goofy...I'm glad I have you guys."

"A-hyuck! Where did that come from?" Goofy wondered.

"It's just...weird, ya know? When I'm with you two, I feel like I can do anything. Don't laugh, but... Well, it almost feels like we've done this before."

The other world with another Sora, data, bugs—Sora still didn't really get it all, but he felt just the tiniest bit of warmth in his chest when he was with these two.

"Well, that right there is a sign you've found true friends!" Donald crossed his arms and said with a nod.

"It's kinda fun to make the same friend twice," Goofy added.

That did sound like fun. Sora wasn't sure what his counterpart in the real world was like, but he had him to thank for friends like these. *I'm me, so that other Sora is and isn't me, I guess. What's he like, I wonder?*

"But right now, it's time to get serious," Donald said with an earnest expression.

"Right! Don't forget, Riku's still waitin' for us!" Goofy continued.

"Okay, c'mon!" Sora called.

At almost that exact moment, the gondola stopped. The wind was howling up here; this was probably the top of the castle.

"That looks like the entrance over there."

Sora and crew climbed up and up, taking out the blocks and Heartless that hindered them along the way.

"Hmm, do ya think it's a dead end?"

"Hey, that looks kinda suspicious down below." Sora peered downward from the high floor they had reached.

"Huh? Where?" Donald poked his head out from behind Sora.

"Can we jump down there?"

As Goofy joined them, the weight of both him and Donald knocked Sora off balance.

"Whoooaaa!"

"Waaak!"

"Waa-hoo-hooey!"

Sora managed to land on his feet, but Donald fell tail-first and Goofy headfirst. Both right on top of him.

"Oh give me a break!" Sora yelped from under his companions.

"Sorry 'bout that."

"Hurry up and move!" Donald squawked as he lifted Goofy's rump off of him. Once the trio was finally back on their feet, they found the entrance to what looked like a dark chamber.

"I don't think anything good happens in there, fellas..." Goofy peeked inside.

"Pete has to be here, don't you think?" Behind him, Donald took a look, too.

"Ready, guys?"

"Of course!"

"Leave it to us!"

The two of them turned to Sora and nodded fiercely. The three friends stepped into the obviously malevolent darkness.

"Gah-ha-ha-ha-ha!" Pete cackled as they arrived.

"We've got you now, Pete!"

Sora strained his eyes against the gloom and saw him standing in middle of a grand hall as if he had been waiting for them.

"Couldn't do a thing by yourself, so you went cryin' to your pals, eh? Well it won't do ya a lick of good!" Pete folded his arms and crowed. He raised his hands, and a group of Heartless appeared all at once.

"Incoming Heartless!"

"Lemme at 'em!"

Donald and Goofy rushed forward to defeat their foes.

"Heh-heh! Gotcha!"

When Pete raised his arm again, a whole slew of blocks rained down on Sora from the empty ceiling.

"Sora!"

"Look out!"

Goofy pushed Sora out of the way, while Donald blasted the blocks dropping from above with his magic.

Unfortunately, it was Donald and Goofy who got caught instead, and the blocks trapped them in a tight, solid wall.

"I can't...move...," Goofy groaned.

"Donald! Goofy!"

Sora called his friends' names, but he couldn't even break the blocks, much less attack Pete. *What should I do? Is there anything I can do?*

"Gah-ha-ha-ha! What a pair of rubes! Why risk your necks for a lump of data? Oh yeah, I know all about this phony. Youse guys made him, just like that phony Keyblade he's got!" Pete sneered at Donald and Goofy in his trap.

"Don't you ever talk about Sora like that. He's our friend in this world and every other one, too!" Donald shouted, wriggling in the tiny space between his body and the wall to strike the blocks with his staff. The wall didn't budge, though.

"Donald..."

I'm so happy to hear you say that, but...I really am useless now.

"Hmph, maybe on the outside, but he's just an empty shell. The kid don't got a heart," Pete continued.

A heart? What's a heart?

"That's not true! We've got Sora's heart right here!" This time, it was Goofy who shouted.

"Oh yeah?" The smile was wiped from Pete's face.

"You'd see it, too, if you were looking. Why would he keep fighting for us—no matter the danger, no matter how hard things got—if he didn't care?" Donald added, poking his face just a bit through one of the gaps in the blocks.

"A-yep!" Goofy agreed. "And we'll fight for him, too. Ya know why? Because he's in our hearts as much as we're in his."

As they declared their unwavering trust, three hearts became one.

"Our friend is our power!"

A warmth spread within Sora's chest like a beacon cutting through the darkness. *My friends are my power.*

"Aww, can the mush! Youse guys are finished." Pete shouted, stamping his foot. "Let's see your 'power' protect you from this!"

The blocks began closing in to crush Donald and Goofy.

"Wak!"

"Yeowch!"

"Donald, no! Goofy!"

What do I do? What can *I do? I can't save them.*

"Nighty-night, losers!"

Pete was hopping up and down. *I can't let this happen! I won't let this be the end of them!*

"Stop... Please, don't hurt them... NO!!!" Sora clenched his fist and punched it into the air—a blinding light engulfed the area.

"What...just...?" Sora mumbled. He couldn't believe what had happened. In his hand was a Keyblade.

The blocks entrapping Donald and Goofy had vanished in the same instant.

"Wh-what's the big idea?! I saw Maleficent destroy that thing!" Flustered, Pete began running around willy-nilly.

At that moment, Sora heard a familiar voice. "Sora, you're just full of surprises!" Mickey came running up.

"Mickey! Why? What did I do?" Sora asked.

"I'm not sure, Sora. All I can say is that something in you has changed. The Keyblade takes its power from the wielder's strength of heart. But an old friend of mine once said, 'A heart is so much more than any system.'" Mickey regarded Sora intently. "I gave you the Keyblade as data, and never expected it to match the real Keyblade's power. I think Maleficent was able to destroy it because it was a copy without true strength."

Sora stared at the Keyblade in his hand.

"But during your journey, you made a connection...with us. You've risen above the system, Sora, and gained power unlike any-body else's. And that's what brought your Keyblade back." Mickey smiled.

"Wow..."

"I guess we were meant to handle this world's bugs together!"

The four of them then glared at Pete.

"This is where it ends, Pete!" Mickey brandished his Keyblade.

"It ain't fair! Sproutin' a new Keyblade is cheating. Better make a strategic retreat, before—"

"Not so fast! First, hand over Riku...or else." Sora readied his Key-blade, too.

"Uhmmm... Now let's *talk* about this..."

Pete was slowly being driven back against the wall. But just then, the world shook.

"Huh? What now?"

The floor shuddered under Sora's feet, and the world around him blinked in and out.

"So long, chumps!" Pete shouted.

Sora tried to go after him, but visibility was poor and the tremors had yet to stop, so he couldn't even walk properly. Finally, he made it to the spot where Pete had been. "No! We lost him!"

He was a few seconds too late, but the scoundrel had left behind a single, solitary clue.

"But we *found* a Keyhole!" Goofy pointed at the object floating above Sora's head.

"Let's head inside!" Donald swung his staff in anticipation.

However, Sora drew his lips in a line and took a step forward. "Hold on, guys," he said quietly. "Leave this one to me."

"Why?" Donald asked back.

"I never would have made it here without the three of you. But it's my turn now. Let me be your light, and I'll show you the way home!"

Donald crossed his arms and looked at Sora out of the corner of his eye while tapping one foot.

"Wh-what is it, Donald?"

"Um, isn't that hamming it up a little? You just wanna test out your new powers, don'tcha?"

"Yeesh… Let me have my moment." Sora scratched his head. Donald was right; he did want to test the power of this "connection" Mickey had talked about. He must be even stronger than he had been before.

"A-hyuck! We'll let it slide this time." Goofy laughed in exasperation.

"You don't have to do this alone, Sora. Remember that you're part of a team. When you get hurt, it hurts us, too," Mickey stated gently.

"How could I forget? I promise I'll come back safe. Now, here I go!"

"See you soon!"

As Mickey and the others looked on, Sora held his Keyblade up to the Keyhole. Light shot from it and into the Keyhole, and there came the *click* of a lock coming undone. Next, a door appeared.

Sora dashed into the opening at top speed.

Within was a chapel with stained glass windows. *Pete can't have gone far*, Sora thought, and sure enough, he spied his foe breathing a sigh of relief at finally getting away.

"End of the road, Pete!"

"Whuh? Don't you know when to quit?"

"Do yourself a favor and come quietly."

"Hmph! After all the times you've ruined my plans? Not likely! It's my turn to teach you a trick or three of my own!"

Pete suddenly rumbled forward and swung down an arm. Sora blocked the powerful blow, but it nearly knocked him back.

"Nngh!"

It was a contest of strength—Pete trying to force his arm down, and Sora trying to hold it in place with his Keyblade.

"You and your puny muscles got nothin' on me!"

"I may not have the muscles, but..."

Sora relaxed his arms on purpose, causing Pete to lose his balance long enough for Sora to jump away and blast him with magic.

"Hmph, not bad, bozo... No more Mr. Nice Pete!"

"And you're gonna wish Mr. Nice Pete was a little nicer!"

Sora closed the distance between them in a flash and lashed out at Pete's belly with his Keyblade.

"Oof... Not again." Pete hunched over, clutching his stomach.

"Give up?"

"Heh! I still gots an ace up my sleeve. Come on out and say hello!" Pete called.

And the one who appeared was...

"Riku?"

Instead of his black coat, Riku was wearing a purple-and-black suit with a strange symbol on it. He seemed like a completely different person.

"Stay back, Sora! Hrrrngh!"

Sora was about to run over to him, but he stopped at Riku's warning. His friend's face was twisted in agony.

"Riku? Wha...what's wrong?"

"I took the liberty of takin' *his* liberty away. All I had to do was load some of those bug thingies into your pally's data-matronics. Now, let's see what my new minion can do. Your master orders you to attack!" Pete said with a smirk.

"Hrgh! Not a chance...," Riku groaned, fighting back.

"Hmm? No dice, eh? Guess we need a little more juice..."

Pete picked up a block from the floor and threw it at Riku, and it vanished into him. Sora remembered that the blocks themselves were bugs. If these blocks were the source of the glitches throughout the worlds, then it would be easy for them to contaminate Riku; he was the personification of the worlds' data.

"Arrrgh!" Riku collapsed to the ground.

"Leave him alone!" Sora yelled, then ran over to Riku and helped him up.

"That oughtta do it. I'll just leave you two to get reacquainted. So long!" Once again, Pete ran off, but now wasn't the time to chase him down. *Riku... I have to help him!*

"Riku! Talk to me!" Sora called out, but there was no response from his fallen friend.

I heard a scream, Sora. What's going on in there?!

Sora could hear Mickey's concerned voice. He raised his head and pleaded desperately. "Mickey, it's Riku! They put bugs in him!"
I can't do anything on my own. I need Mickey's help...but how?!

What?! Riku, can you hear me? Riku!

As if Mickey's thoughts had reached him, Riku opened his eyes.

"C'mon, Riku!"

But Riku began to drag himself away from Sora, almost like he was trying to run from him, and then leaped back. Surprised by the sudden movement, Sora looked at his friend. Riku was frozen, staring fixedly at the ground as if he was fighting something within himself.

"Can't you hear us...?"

"Nngh... Strike me...down..."

"What?"

Before Sora could ask him more about what he meant, Riku fired a blast of magic from his hand.

"Riku!"

Sora swiftly dodged the spell, but Riku could easily read such a simple motion. He closed the distance between them all at once and attacked.

"Stop it, Riku!"

Sora was a goner at this rate. *I have to find a way to stop him...!*

Knocking aside his friend's blows, Sora delivered a series of strikes with his Keyblade that only hurt him a little.

"I'm sorry, Riku!" He swung the Keyblade wide and hard, and Riku went flying through the air and crashed to the ground.

"...Riku!"

Some of the red-and-black blocks began to emerge from Riku's body. They were in there deep—how could he get them out?

As Sora plopped down on the floor in exhaustion from the battle, a powerful light shone behind him.

"Sora! Riku!" Mickey and the others appeared from the beam. "Well, if the bugs have taken over Riku...then that means...he might not ever wake up—unless we get rid of the bugs first," the king explained, gazing at Riku in concern.

"So if I debug him, Riku will come back to us. Guys, I gotta go inside to look," Sora said with unwavering determination as he knelt down beside his friend.

"But what about you?!"

"Who's to say if it's even safe inside Riku?"

Worried, Donald and Goofy tried to stop their friend.

"I know it's risky. But if a friend needs me to be there, I'll be there—to help!" Sora looked at Mickey, Donald, Goofy, and Jiminy in turn. "I want to help everyone."

Their expressions softened.

"Well, I guess that's Sora for ya," Jiminy commented, both happy and a little chagrined.

"Still can't talk you out of it, huh?" Donald shook his head with a smile, too.

"A-hyuck! But we'll do everything we can to help you out!" Goofy gave Sora a hard slap on the back.

"Thanks, guys."

A smile appeared on Sora's face, and he gathered the strength to stand.

"I'm going."

The four nodded deeply, and Sora held the Keyblade out toward Riku's chest. A Keyhole rose out of his body, and a door opened.

"Sora, don't forget—you're not going in there alone," Mickey assured him. "Your friends'll be right there fighting alongside ya in spirit, no matter where ya go."

Sora smiled as he ran into the light.

CHAPTER 8
Reverse/Rebirth

SORA STEPPED INTO THE WORLD WITHIN RIKU—PERHAPS it was best to call this place a datascape of Jiminy's journal, for which Riku served as the vessel. It was dark, with wires of light occasionally racing across the gloom.

"It's so…empty," Sora whispered uneasily, looking at his feet. Suddenly, a shock ran through him, as if something very heavy had been dropped onto his shoulders.

"Aaah!" Sora cried as a ball of light shot out of him. The burden on his shoulders remained. His knees felt like they were about to give out under him.

"Wh-what's going on? I feel k-kinda funny."

It was like the energy had been sucked right out of him. What just happened?

"Sora! You okay?" Riku came running up.

"Riku! What about you? Are you all right?"

Sora was still worried for his friend, though his legs were so wobbly he could barely stand.

Riku gave him a small nod in reply. "You shouldn't be here. I can fight the bugs off a little longer…but they're spreading. Pretty soon they'll take over all my data."

The bugs were starting to win. What would happen once their control was complete?

"You feel weak, right? It's because the bugs have stolen your data. You won't last long in here. Take this and escape while you can." Riku held out a strange glowing shard.

"What is it?"

Sora peered at the item in Riku's hand. Inside the dull light, he saw several glimmers of something that had a stronger glow. He had no idea what it was, though.

"Data I found on my other partition. It doesn't belong in Jiminy's journal. Somebody added it after the fact."

Sora took the fragment and held it overhead to give it a closer look, but he couldn't discern anything special. What could be hidden in this extra data?

"The same person that hid the journal's contents inside you?"

"I'm not sure. It's up to you now to find out," said Riku. "Thanks to you, all the bugs outside of me are gone. If you can just solve the mystery of this extra data, then the journal will be completely restored. That should open the way back for Mickey and the others."

Riku's saying to leave him here? No, I can't do that. "But what about you?!" Sora exclaimed.

"I'll dive into the darkness and take these bugs with me. They'll never see the light again," Riku stated resolutely before Sora could continue. He smiled softly.

But...I don't want to just leave him behind. Sora lowered his gaze.

"Go, Sora. While I'm still in control. The bugs are getting stronger, but there's still just enough time."

"Well, then...I guess that settles it." *Why does he always do this?* Sora gave him a long look.

"Right." Riku nodded quietly. "So you better—"

"If there's just enough time to escape, then there's just enough time to stop the bugs. We can beat this, Riku!" With a grin, Sora presented the solution he'd found.

"What? You're not listening!" Riku flinched.

"Heh-heh! Come on, Riku. You didn't really think I'd just give up and leave?" As Sora laughed, Riku let out a big sigh.

"Sora, I... Ugh, why do I bother? Once you get an idea in your head, that's it."

Riku smiled, too.

Yep, I'm as stubborn as they come. "Well, at least you learned to stop trying! That's progress!"

"All right. Well, the bugs have stolen your powers, so the first thing you've gotta do is get them back."

Riku held up his hand, palm-out, and a door appeared leading to some unknown destination. The other side looked full of blinding light, perhaps because the place where they were now was so dark.

"That light over there leads deeper into my data. Inside is a world from my memories..."

"Your memories?"

"Yeah, that's right. The memories of the data version of me. And some of the bugs that stole your data. Get the data back, get your powers back. It's simple. *Then* you can worry about me. Be careful."

"Okay. Be right back!" Sora nodded and stepped toward the light.

"Good luck in there. And thanks."

"Any time!" Still smiling, Sora stepped through the beaming doorway without a moment's hesitation.

Before him were the Destiny Islands. Sora yelped at the state they were in. "Yeesh. What a mess!"

His home was covered in blocks, and the once refreshing breeze from the ocean was unpleasant. It felt like each step was draining his strength. If he didn't get his powers back, even just walking forward would be difficult.

Sora swung his Keyblade at the block in front of him. It disappeared like normal, but this time he also felt a sliver of his strength return. So getting rid of the blocks would restore him.

"Okay, I can do this!"

Sora tore through all the blocks around him. His body still felt like lead, but he could tell that his strength was finding its way home bit by bit. After cleaning the beach, he ran over the bridge to the little island. Once the bugs there were gone, he would be done.

"And that's that!"

The Destiny Islands were now bug-free. *Okay, what next?*

As Sora stood there wondering, Riku appeared.

"Riku?"

"I can access this world now that you've weakened the bugs. It's our island..." Riku took in the view of the sea.

"Yeah... Hey, remember when you gave me the Keyhole?"

Though it felt like ages ago, it had happened only recently.

"You needed a chance to prove yourself with the Keyblade—and learn how things work in the datascape." Riku turned to Sora.

"Yeah, the riddles were a nice touch. Did you know I was gonna have to fight that thing inside?"

"Sink or swim. Sorry. The clock was ticking. Inside the journal, the Heartless had already shattered the walls between worlds, and now the wall between the datascape and the real world was under attack from the bugs. I used that to my advantage and called Mickey and the others here to help."

Riku lowered his gaze for just a moment.

"Some kind of…mysterious message, right?" Sora replied lightly. "Not much progress there."

He started to think. He'd debugged all kinds of worlds, but there were still plenty of mysteries left.

"I shouldn't have dragged everybody into this without asking." Riku seemed to deeply regret his actions.

"Well, no big deal, as long as we get them home," Sora reassured him with a smile and a shrug. "So whaddaya say? Back to work?"

"Right. Come with me," Riku replied, and then they blinked away.

Sora's next point of arrival was Traverse Town. Just as with the Destiny Islands, the streets were blanketed in blocks. Sora destroyed them one after the other, and he could feel more of his strength returning with each one gone. He hurried through the town until all had been eliminated.

And like on the islands, Riku appeared before Sora when he was done.

"Looks like you've taken care of the bugs here, too."

"Riku!"

"Thanks, Sora. Last time I was here, it was to keep the triplets safe," Riku commented, reminiscing.

"Huey, Dewey, and Louie?" Sora remembered those three rambunctious brothers very well.

"Right. They had the pieces of the Keyhole, which made them targets. Somebody had to look out for them."

I didn't know anything about that. Sora pursed his lips unhappily. "Riku, why didn't you just tell me what was going on?"

"You still needed to toughen up a little on your own. You had a difficult job ahead, and if you couldn't do it..." Riku lowered his gaze. "Well, I guess I would've been on my own."

Sora let out a heavy sigh. *Some things never change.* "Riku, you always try to take everything on by yourself," he said, and Riku looked up. "But I *like* getting dragged into your messes. Donald and Goofy said the same thing to me."

"Maybe so, but—"

"Forget this 'on my own' talk already."

I know Riku didn't have anyone to help him deal with all this complicated stuff back then, but he's not alone anymore. That's why it makes me sad to hear him talk about doing everything by himself. I mean, it kinda starts to feel like I'm the only one who thinks we're friends.

"Sorry... You're right."

"And stop saying you're sorry. We've got better things to do! You ready?"

Sora laughed, but Riku's expression was still glum as they headed for the next world.

Wonderland, too, was infested with blocks. Once again, Riku arrived once they were all gone.

"Sora... Really, I'm sor—"

"Nope! Don't say it!"

Even after all this, Riku was still downcast.

"Can you blame me? I shouldn't have let the bugs in like this. Every time it's me against some outside force, I give in and—" Riku gazed at the palm of his hand.

I get that you're worried, but this isn't like you, Riku. "Riku, would you can it for a second?" Sora said. "How many worlds have we been to now? A whole bunch, right?"

"Yeah..." Riku closed his palm into a fist.

"Well, not long ago, the answer would have been 'one.' But now, you and me have been all kinds of places. Instead of dreaming about what's out there, we only have to remember it. We've got the whole universe inside of us."

Sora thought back on the worlds they had visited on their journeys. *There are all kinds of worlds out there, and plenty of them we've never seen.*

"Just let that sink in for a second."

"...Pretty incredible."

Riku nodded, and Sora continued.

"All those worlds inside you, and you know what? You're still Riku. Doesn't matter how many 'outside forces' you have to face—because everything you touch makes you stronger. Always has."

"Th-thanks." Riku finally raised his head and looked at Sora.

"Heh-heh, you like that? Sounded wise beyond my years, right?"

Sora chuckled, a little bashfully, and Riku finally smiled along with him. "A little flowery, but you made your point, half-pint."

"H-hey! I'll remember that when I'm taller than you!" Sora shot back. That was low!

Riku burst into laughter, as if he couldn't hold it in anymore, and Sora joined in.

"Ha-ha! I look forward to *that*." Riku's laughter subsided, and he looked at Sora again. "And Sora?"

"Yeah?"

Riku seemed to want to say something, but then he gave a small shake of his head. "...Never mind. I'll tell you when all this is over."

"Sure, okay—when I see you on the other side. This next one is the last, right?"

"Yeah."

Riku nodded, and the pair disappeared from Wonderland.

The final place Sora arrived was the interior of the cave in Agrabah. Not only was it packed to the gills with blocks, but Sora also had to work through the bevy of traps in the cavern, all the way from the depths to the exit. Quite a bit of his power was back now, and Sora dashed through the cave barely breaking a sweat. He still wasn't fully restored, but he was light-years better than he'd been while squashing the bugs on the Destiny Islands.

Outside the cave, he destroyed all the blocks in front of the great tiger's head, too.

"Riku!"

Sora ran up to his friend as he arrived like always.

"Remember this place?" Riku said, ever so slightly wistful.

"Yeah. This is where Maleficent ambushed me. If it wasn't for you, I'd have been a goner."

What would have happened to me then if Riku and Mickey hadn't been there?

"Mickey and I knew Pete had another trick up his sleeve."

Maleficent destroyed my Keyblade back then. "Well, it was a good one. I lost my Keyblade," Sora said softly, then grinned. "But see, that just proves things are gonna work out!"

"Um, how?" Riku asked.

"No matter what you lose, you can always get it back. And that means you can get yourself back!" Sora declared confidently.

Riku shook his head a bit and smiled in amazement. "Heh. Sometimes I envy how simple your world is."

"Is...that a compliment?" Sora asked in mild protest.

"I envy whatever makes you think it could be."

"Gee, thanks," Sora remarked as Riku snickered.

"Ha-ha-ha. Race ya back"

"H-hey, wait up!"

Riku vanished first with a laugh, with Sora hurriedly following his lead.

When Sora and Riku returned to the dim realm, a shining entrance lay before them.

"Okay. Enough of the hurt as been undone for you to access the innermost reaches of my data."

Riku pointed out the new doorway.

"In there is the source of all the other sources of bugs. Be careful—we don't know what it is, where it came from, or why it's really here."

"No… But we know that taking it out will clear up the last of the datascape's problems. Right?"

Sora glared at the door a little.

"Right. Everything should go back to the way it was," said Riku, facing the entrance with similar determination.

Sora turned to his friend. "Thanks for all this, Riku. I feel like going through your memories has made me stronger."

"You don't have to thank me."

"Sure I do! You've guided me the whole way."

Actually, come to think of it, Riku was there when I woke up for the first time. I should thank him for that, too.

"You were even there when I first woke up, when I first got the Keyblade."

But Riku seemed confused. "Huh? No, the first time I saw you was on our island."

"What? But I'm sure I saw you there… In your black coat? Huh. That's weird."

Sora was sure that he had encountered someone in a black coat there, too. If it was someone else wearing the same thing, then who would it have been?

"Well, stay focused," Riku said. "Are you ready for this fight? I can't go in with you."

Sora looked up at him.

"About all I can tell you is not to hold back, no matter what you see in there."

There was something Riku wasn't telling him—maybe he knew what was waiting beyond the door.

"Huh? Okay… Wish me luck." Sora took a step toward the doorway.

Behind him, Riku repeated his advice. "Just remember what I said."

"Don't hold back, no matter what I see. I got it," Sora replied, then entered the door.

"Just…be careful, Sora," Riku said softly.

On the other side of the glowing entryway was the chapel of Hollow Bastion, along with…

"Riku?!" Sora shouted. "But how—?"

Riku was wearing the black-and-purple suit he'd had while under Pete's control.

"No… You're not him."

Sora quickly realized that the one before him was both Riku and not Riku—a bug that had siphoned his power to take his form.

"That explains the warnings," Sora whispered, then readied his Keyblade. He wasn't afraid of a fake Riku. It was just a bug. Sora lunged forward and closed the distance.

Though it had been standing there apparently in a daze, the bug blocked Sora's attack. It then jumped back to fire off a series of shining white fireballs.

"Urgh!"

Despite Sora's attempts to deflect each of the flaming orbs that assailed him, one of them hit him dead-on and sent him flying.

Sora did have most of his power back, but he still wasn't at 100 percent. The powerful attack hit him hard, and it took all his strength to withstand it. He wasn't ready to lose just yet, though. Sora got up and immediately cast a spell that created the opening he needed to land a flurry of blows on the bug.

As his enemy fell still and disappeared, Sora could feel all his strength returning to him. *That means all the bugs must be gone!*

Sora struck a macho pose—and then realized he was back in that dark space.

"You did it! Nice work, Sora." Riku met Sora with a smile.

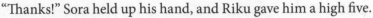

"Thanks!" Sora held up his hand, and Riku gave him a high five.

"The bug tried to use my power for itself, didn't it?"

"Yeah... How'd you know?" Sora asked in return.

Riku's expression darkened slightly. "Just one of those gut feelings. I thought it might try to exploit the darkness inside me." Riku paused briefly, then smiled with a hint of sadness. "Maybe...I've been a little jealous. You're always surrounded by friends who trust you and are there to support you—"

But Sora wasn't having it. "Okay, stop right there. First of all, *I* trust you. Second of all, my friends are your friends, too. Just ask 'em!"

Riku! Sora! Are you two all right in there?

They immediately heard Mickey's voice.

Squish some bugs for me, would ya?

There was Donald.

A-hyuck! Just holler if ya need some help!

And finally Goofy. All three of them were Sora and Riku's dear friends.

"Heh-heh. Okay, you win." Riku nodded, then lowered his head and smiled.

"C'mon. They're all waiting for us!" Sora declared. But then an ominous tremor rocked the area. The lights coursing through the air flickered intensely, and the world shook.

"Um, Riku...?"

"No!" Riku's head whipped back and forth. "Sora, you've got to escape, right now! Someone's trying to close the road back to the outside world!"

The tremors were getting so bad it was hard to even stand.

"Hurry, or you'll be trapped in here!" Riku held out his hand, and a black portal appeared. "Go now!" he said, then grabbed Sora by the arm and pulled him over to it.

"O-o-okay, I'm going!"

"Thanks again," Riku told him as he headed into the gate. "I'll see you on the other side!"

"That's a promise!"

Sora turned back and waved, then dashed into the door. This black space was a strange realm. There were blocks moving around that got in his way, but Sora wouldn't make any progress at all if he didn't use the animated obstacles.

He made his way forward, clambering over blocks and defeating Heartless all the while, until he reached someone standing in his path.

"Maleficent!"

"You should have stayed outside, boy. There, the worst fate to befall you would have been eternal slumber."

"You did that?! Yeesh. When are you gonna quit?" Sora retorted, holding his Keyblade up for a fight.

"Oh, I've only just begun. Such a shame you understand so little of the darkness. The world desires its embrace!" The evil fairy lifted her staff slightly.

"Yeah, right."

"There is nothing in darkness," Maleficent reverently intoned. "No sadness, no cause for hurt… In darkness, one cannot see one's mistakes or the dreams that failed to be."

"And they'll never know happiness, either, or what it is to have fun! You can't force the darkness on a world that never asked for it. That's just giving yourself what *you* want!"

That sounds absolutely awful. What's so great about a world where you can't see any of the fun in it?

"And what is wrong with that? After all, the Mistress of All Evil has the right…and the power to see it done!"

Maleficent made a large circle with her staff, and a strange green flame rose up around her.

"If you won't listen to reason, I'll have to stop you by force," Sora declared. Not to be outdone, he made a mighty swing of his Keyblade.

"At last, we agree. I shall put a stop to your meddling here and now!"

Maleficent's brilliant aura of emerald light flared up, and she transformed into a gigantic black dragon that belched green fire toward Sora.

"...Aggh!"

Sora deftly rolled across the ground, away from the blaze and underneath her enormous body, and thrust his Keyblade up from below. Dragon Maleficent roared and stomped across the floor. However, Sora leaped onto her back, sprinted up her long neck, and swung his Keyblade down on her head.

"Graaah!"

His adversary fell still with a terrible screech.

"You can't have this world!" Sora cried. With a mighty leap, he again brought his Keyblade down onto the dragon's head, this time with every ounce of strength he had. Wreathed in green flame, the dragon transformed back into Maleficent.

"All worlds are mine, boy! One day you shall see..." With those parting words, Maleficent staggered off and spirited herself away, through a large door that had materialized behind her.

It was finally over. Beyond the door was Hollow Bastion—specifically, the great hall where Sora had reclaimed his Keyblade and gone to save Riku.

"Sora! He's back, fellas!" Goofy gave Sora a tackle-hug.

"'Bout time! Goofy was worried." Donald latched on from the other side.

"Hey, cut it out, guys!"

Smiling, Mickey walked up to Sora before his two friends could squeeze the air out of him. "Welcome back, Sora. I sure am glad you're not hurt. Well, good news: you did it! The last of the bugs has been wiped from the datascape. I can't thank you enough."

"Always happy to help. Hey! Where's Riku? Is he okay?!" Sora exclaimed, removing himself from his friends' tight grip. *There's no point if Riku didn't make it back.*

Riku quietly stepped into view. "Fine. Sorry to put you through all that."

"There you are!"

Riku offered a hand to Sora and helped him up. "Looks like we managed to keep that promise. I wish we had the time to sit around and chat, but Mickey and the others need to hurry. This way, guys. As promised, here's your road home to the real world." He pointed, and a large door appeared.

"Then this is it…time to say good-bye to the datascape," Mickey said soberly.

"Truth be told, I'm sad to go. It sure was something to explore the inside of my journal!" Jiminy reflected from atop Mickey's shoulder.

"Well, you can come back anytime!" Sora called out from behind Mickey and the rest as they stood before the door.

"Yep! Hey, next time, let's bring the whole gang!"

"That sounds like fun!"

Goofy and Donald seemed happy.

"Actually…," Riku said quietly, "there's something important I haven't told you. Now that… Well, it's just…" He seemed to be having trouble finishing the thought.

"What's the matter, Riku?"

"You know what? I shouldn't keep you any longer. I can tell you after you've made it through," Riku replied with a shake of his head.

Actually, Riku had something he needed to say earlier, too. I wonder what he wants us to know?

"Well…all right. Thanks for all your help! You two take care now." Mickey said his farewells, giving Sora and Riku each a nod.

"We'll see you soon!"

"See ya!"

Donald, Goofy, and Jiminy followed Mickey through the door. Once they were on the other side, the door vanished in a burst of light.

"Yahoo! They're back!"

"Welcome home, everybody!"

Chip and Dale were hopping atop the big desk.

"Chip and Dale are here…"

"And that means…"

Donald and Goofy embraced.

"We made it! Our real castle in the real world!" Jiminy exclaimed, hopping just as excitedly.

> *Looks like it worked. Can you all hear me?*

Everyone looked up at the voice from the monitor.

"Clear as a bell, Riku! Boy, what would we do without you guys?" Mickey replied to the screen.

> *Yeah, about that… Me and Sora here can't help you guys anymore.*

Riku's voice was very quiet.

"Huh? Whaddaya mean?" Donald waddled quickly up to the monitor.

> *With the bugs gone, the journal will revert to its original state. That much isn't news, right?*

"Right. It should return to the way it was when I wrote it." Jiminy elaborated on Riku's explanation.

*　　*　　*

Well, that's the thing... Sora and I will also be reset. We won't remember any of this. After all, there's no mention in the journal of the fight to repair the bugs.

"Wait... You mean you'll forget about all this time we were together? Even the stuff we're talking about right now?" Donald exclaimed sadly.

We're data. That's the way it goes.

After Riku laid out the facts, Goofy sat down dejectedly. "But that's not fair!"

Mickey, still there?

The next voice they heard was Sora's.

Riku explained this to me ahead of time. We should be celebrating! This is how our world is supposed to be.

"Yeah, but still." Donald glumly bowed his head.
　　"You went through so much to help us! Taking all that away isn't right!" Jiminy sadly removed his top hat and held it against his chest.

You're a good friend, Jiminy. Don't worry. You won't get rid of us that easily. We might lose some memories, but we've still got you guys. And whatever part of us doesn't stay in the journal will always stay inside you, right? The worlds may be gone, but never the memories. You can hang onto them for us. Just keep us in your hearts, and we'll be there when you need us most.

Jiminy sniffled.
　　"Oh, Sora..."

Donald and Goofy called out his name at almost the same time.

> *Well, we should sign off here. Good-bye. Give the "us" out there our best!*

Just as Sora was saying farewell, the glitch alarm sounded from the analyzer.

"Wh-what's that?!" Donald's head swiveled around anxiously.

The monitor instantly went black, and a cryptic message appeared on the screen.

> *DATA RECOVERY... 100%*
> *DATA ASSEMBLY COMPLETE*

"What does this mean?" Mickey grimly read the words on the monitor.

> *GLITCH FOUND IN DARKNESS.*
> *AWAKENING DARK GLITCH.*
> *DELETE DATASCAPE YES/NO?*
> *YES*

Back in the great hall of Hollow Bastion, Sora and Riku found themselves in the middle of a horrific quake. All around them they could hear a shrill noise, as if the entire world was screaming under the strain.

"Do you feel that? It's a bug! No it's...it's controlling the bugs. Making them go crazy!"

> *Bugs?! But I thought we got rid of all those!*

They could hear Goofy's voice overhead. Hadn't they done away with all the bugs? Or did this mean that some were left?

"I don't know! Maybe we missed some?" Riku sounded tense.

*   *   *

What are we gonna do?

Donald sounded panicked.

"It said it was going to delete the datascape. We can't let something this big get loose. Lock the journal data! Hurry!" Riku directed Mickey back in the real world.

> *But…if we do, we'll lose you and Sora,* and *what was in the journal!*

Before Mickey was finished talking, Jiminy yelped, too.

> *Ah! Oh, dear, I just remembered! Maleficent and Pete are still inside! They'll be deleted, too!*

I forgot all about those two. They should definitely still be in here. And if the journal was locked, they'd be lost along with all the data.

> *Evil or not, we can't let that happen!*

At Mickey's words, Riku bit his lip. "Then locking the data isn't an option?" He groaned. "The real world is at stake!"

Next to him, Sora stared directly ahead. At this rate, it was all going to be for nothing. *I have no choice but to go.*

"Hang tight, guys! Just give me a little time!"

"Wait, Sora! Where are you going? Sora!" Riku grabbed Sora by the arm as he started to run off. "The datascape won't hold together much longer! Sora, stop!"

Sora had no intention of doing that.

"Sora, are you crazy?" Riku urged, still with a firm grip on his friend's arm.

"We can't just leave them! You heard Mickey. I'm going to find them!"

"Find them where?! Do you have any idea where they are?"

"Somewhere!" Sora snapped.

Riku took hold of Sora by both shoulders and gazed into his eyes in an effort to get through to him. Sora stared right back.

"Aren't you afraid?" Riku asked softly. "We're not just talking about losing some memories here. We could get erased. This whole world could get erased!"

"Sure I'm afraid. Weren't you?"

"Hmm?"

Sora slowly removed Riku's hands. "You've been in my shoes. You've gone up against the impossible alone. Because you knew that was less scary than just sitting around and waiting for the end." *What's scary is doing nothing. Not trying. Going into the void without a fight.* "I don't know if we can win—but I know I've gotta try. There's no telling what will happen next. But now is the time to get out there and do something!"

"—There really is no stopping you once you get something in your head." Riku gave him the barest hint of a smile.

"Same goes for you! Let me take care of this!"

> *LONG HAVE THE FALLEN WANDERED.*
> *NOW THEY SHALL SERVE THE WILL OF DARKNESS.*

It was that strange voice again. Sora didn't know whom it belonged to, but he had the feeling he'd heard it somewhere before. In that same moment, a glowing door appeared before him.

"It's in your hands now, Sora."

With Riku's voice at his back, Sora ran into the portal.

Within lay a strange path that seemed to stretch on forever. Sora hurried down the road, taking down any swarms of Heartless that tried to cut him off.

He could see a light farther ahead. It got brighter and brighter, and when it was almost too bright for him to look at, he found himself standing in a bizarre realm.

"Uhh, Maleficent? We don't seem to be makin' much progress here…"

"Hmph! Any less of an opponent would be an insult."

Pete and Maleficent were fending off a giant Heartless with attack after attack, but there wasn't any indication that their efforts were having an effect. This one bore a strong resemblance to the enormous Darkside Sora had fought on the Destiny Islands way back in the beginning.

Maybe it didn't vanish back then because the darkness swallowed us both together.

Sora ran in front of Pete and Maleficent.

"Maleficent! Pete! You two need to get out of here!" Sora told them with his Keyblade at the ready.

"I do not take orders from you!"

"Uh…I vote we listen to this pipsqueak."

"Silence, coward! You will do as I say!" Maleficent waved her staff angrily. The emerald fire from it hit the second incarnation of that giant Heartless—Neo Darkside—but there were no visible signs of any damage. Not flinching in the slightest, Neo Darkside raised a huge arm and slammed its fist into the ground.

"What?!"

Maleficent and Pete were gone. Had they been crushed under the blow?

"Pete! Maleficent!" Sora cried.

Neo Darkside looked down at Sora coolly. The boy wavered for a second, overcome by its intense presence. The Heartless had an overwhelmingly intimidating aura, far worse than during his first confrontation with it. This was virtually something else altogether.

RAGE… HATRED… AND NOW GLITCHES TO FEED MY DARKNESS.

Sora sensed that the voice was coming from Neo Darkside. It fed on glitches?

*   *   *

 Wait…that's it! You're not the only one who evolved within the datascape!

Sora looked up as he heard Riku's voice.
 "Riku, you wanna fill me in?"
What Riku told Sora next was very hard to take in all at once.

 I know where the bugs came from—all of them! It's your shadow—your Heartless!

"My Heartless?!" Sora shouted in disbelief. *I had a Heartless?!*

 You may not remember it, but you were turned into a Heartless once. That was written in the journal. But those records vanished along with your memories not long after your first journey. You got your memories back, but the pages of the journal—they stayed blank.

"And you think my Heartless is responsible?"
 Sora didn't understand exactly what Riku was saying. Still, he was pretty sure the gist of it was that his own Heartless was the cause of all the bugs.

 It makes sense. Everything in the journal revolved around you. This whole time you've been evolving in the datascape—finding new strength—your Heartless has been absorbing data and doing the same.

"But we put all the data back! That weakened it, right? I can still stop it!" Sora took his Keyblade in hand and faced Neo Darkside once more.

 No…I should have realized sooner. Normally defeating Heartless releases hearts, which then return to the people who lost them. Defeating Heartless here in the datascape, though—that wouldn't have set any real hearts free. Instead, you released the Heartless' minds.

"Their minds? Well, where did those end up?"

Sora didn't understand as much about hearts and Heartless, or how the world worked, as Riku. *What exactly is going on here? Are the hearts and minds of Heartless really that different?*

> *Right in front of you! Your Heartless has been gathering, then devouring the dark intentions of the fallen Heartless. That's where it gets its power: dark data! And now, just like you, it's become something greater.*

My Heartless—and now it's something new. There's no telling what would happen to Mickey and the others—to everyone in the entire world—if this guy ever made it out of here.

"I have to protect them. And with all the strength they've given me, I can!"

As if responding to his voice, Neo Darkside looked at Sora. With a snarl, it shot beams of light from its chest into the sky. The rays arced up and over, turning into a rain around Sora.

"Ugh!"

Sora tried threading through the downpour toward Neo Darkside, but this time it pounded the ground with its fist.

Sora hopped backward and swung his Keyblade down on its arm.

Neo Darkside appeared to pause for a moment, but then it thrust both arms toward the heavens and sent a wave of light from its body. Sora deflected it with his Keyblade, then charged straight into the Heartless's chest and hammered it with a series of blows until it fell still.

"Is it over?!"

Just as he struck a victory pose, that voice sounded in his head again.

＊　＊　＊

RAGE... HATRED... GLITCHES TO FEED MY DARK-NESS...
AND SOON, HEARTS TO SATE MY HUNGER!

"What is it? It's changing again?! No... It's evolving!"

What stood before him looked exactly like him—well, almost. The profile and size were the same, but it was entirely black. This really was Sora's Heartless.

It held its own Keyblade aloft, with three other Keyblades orbiting around it. Each of the dangerous-looking weapons was steeped in darkness.

"What the heck is this?!"

The trio of Keyblades attacked Sora repeatedly, but he managed to evade them long enough to get close and strike his Heartless. After several similar exchanges, Sora landed a series of hits that took all he could muster.

And yet those glowing eyes in the darkness seemed eerily mirthful. The creature floated into the air and summoned a slew of darkness-infused Keyblades around its body.

"What?!"

The black Keyblades descended on Sora all at once, as another—golden, this time—rose up above the Heartless's head. The golden Keyblade carved a line through the air toward Sora.

But Sora deftly struck the golden copy to the ground with his own Keyblade, then picked it up and threw it back at his Heartless. A direct hit.

Its strength exhausted, Sora's Heartless shrank—all the way down into a Shadow. Shadows were a weak little Heartless; he'd defeated plenty of them in the past. In fact, it was the first type of Heartless he'd beat on the Destiny Islands. Sora brought his Keyblade down on the feebly squirming creature.

"Did *that* do it?!"

But when Sora started to relax—his Heartless appeared again. Only now there were three of them.

The boy fought them desperately, as he had before, and eventually they fell, only for yet another trio to take their place. Sora was beginning to falter now, but he rallied his wavering heart and battled on. And just when he thought he had gotten the last of them—Neo Darkside returned.

"When is this gonna end?!"

It was enough to make him want to throw in the towel, even if his legs weren't literally giving out under him. He had no idea how long the struggle had been going on. Sora collapsed to his knees, and he could feel consciousness slipping away.

What's happening to me? Falling—into darkness…

"You can't give up!"

Sora looked up at the familiar, reassuring voice. Standing there was—*Mickey!*

"Mickey? What are you doing here?" Sora felt new strength welling up in his exhausted body.

"Helping my friend. Didn't I tell ya? You never have to face things alone."

Sora slowly got to his feet. *He's right; I'm not alone. Everyone's here with me.*

"When the darkness closes in, just look inside—and you'll always find your light!"

Mickey fired a beam from his Keyblade into the heart-shaped hollow in Neo Darkside's torso. As the powerful light swallowed it, the great Heartless transformed before their eyes into a lone Shadow.

"C'mon! It's time!" Sora chopped down with his Keyblade, and the Shadow was gone without a trace. "We did it!" he cheered as the world filled with light. That should be the last of the bugs.

The glow enfolded Sora and Mickey as well—and before they knew it, they were back in the great hall of Hollow Bastion. Maleficent and Pete stood off in one corner. Riku was there, too, of course.

"Pete! Maleficent! You're all right!" Sora called.

Riku smiled at him. "I found them caught in a rift in the data," he said with a shrug.

Maleficent scowled bitterly. "Hmph! You will hear no words of thanks from me. Our debt is settled."

"I was fixin' to get out of here already! So long, chumps. I'm goin' home!" Pete began to stomp off, but you had to wonder if he really knew the way out. Maleficent followed after him.

"I'll keep an eye on them on their way out." Riku urged them on ahead.

"Next time, youse guys are in for it!" Pete snapped at them.

Sora and Mickey shared a glance.

"Ha-ha! Pete will never change."

"Nope."

Smiling, the two turned to face each other.

"The data will start returning to normal soon. The way it was before those bugs showed up," Mickey said.

"Then I guess this time it's good-bye for real." Sora made a fist over his chest. "...Huh? What gives? This lump in my throat... Is it another glitch?" *I feel sad, somehow. What is this...?*

"No, Sora. That's just what good-byes feel like."

Sora's hand remained where it was as he listened to what Mickey had to say.

"Gosh... Our time together brought back a whole flood of memories. The day I set out on my first adventure. The day I made a new friend."

A flood of memories... What did Mickey's memories hold?

"It made me realize that the journal isn't just a list of events. It's a collection of everything we felt together—it's our hearts."

Hearts couldn't be turned to data...but the journal was a collection of them...?

"I promise we'll tell Sora and Riku what happened here. That way, this journey will be one we can share with you. Those memories will always keep our hearts connected."

That's right! If our hearts connect and form a bond, that connection will last even if the memories are gone.

"Friends forever, Sora!"

Mickey held out his right hand to Sora.

"Friends forever, Mick—Your Majesty."

Sora unclenched his hand and held it out to the king, and the two of them shared a firm handshake.

"Okay, I'm off."

Mickey started walking toward the door of light.

Once Mickey had disappeared into the glow and Sora was sure Mickey was on the other side, he held out his Keyblade to the door. The familiar beam of light locked it tight.

And then…

Donald, Goofy, Jiminy, Chip, and Dale greeted Mickey upon his return to Disney Castle.

"What's that?!"

Jiminy pointed at the monitor, where they saw a message from Sora.

THANKS, GUYS!

CHAPTER 9
Castle Oblivion

Hey, do you remember?

The mood in the study of Disney Castle was relatively relaxed and relieved. The adventure was at an end, and the Sora in the datascape had lost all memory of the journey. The monitor of the computer analyzing the journal only displayed the book's actual contents.

"Hey, ya know...we never did figure out that mysterious message," Goofy remarked from where he stood next to the king's chair.

On the other side, Donald let out a long sigh. They had gotten rid of the bugs for good, but they hadn't accomplished what they'd originally set out to do.

Suddenly, tension was in the air again, and Donald was the first to notice why.

"Wak!"

Riku had appeared on the monitor.

> *Guys, big news. A new world has shown up inside the journal.*

"What do you mean?" Goofy asked curiously.

> *I've found another door leading to extra data. Somebody must have added it once all the other data was restored.*

"And if we explore that world..."

> *...Then we should get some answers about this message.*

Riku finished Mickey's sentence.

> *Their hurting will be mended when you return to end it.*

* * *

The strange message appeared on the screen again. Who were "they"? What was hurting them?

"Great!" Mickey started to rise from his seat. "Let's ask Sora to—"

"When we fixed the data, everything in the journal went back to the way it started, remember?" said Goofy with a hint of sadness. Donald sighed next to Mickey on the other side.

"Which means Sora's journey through the datascape—it never happened to him. Why, now he's just the same boy he was before he met any of us," Jiminy quietly confirmed. Now that the journal had been completely restored, Sora's memory had returned to how it was before his journey—now, he only remembered the Destiny Islands.

I'm fine; my partition isn't affected. But Sora—we can't send him out there when he doesn't know what's going on.

Riku looked worried on the screen.

Mickey thought for a moment. "Wait. Hey, Riku," he said. "Could you help me get back in the datascape one more time?"

Donald, Goofy, and Jiminy all turned toward Mickey.

Pluto licked Sora's face. He was lying unconscious in an alleyway; only a little bit of light was shining around the corner.

"Unh…" Sora opened his bleary eyes slowly, but what he saw was not the ocean of the Destiny Islands nor the sky overhead, but a town he'd never seen before—and a dog.

"What a dream…," Sora muttered, then closed his eyes again—until Pluto jumped on his stomach.

"Ungh—this isn't a dream!"

Sora stood and rubbed his eyes, then took a look around him. *What is this place…?*

Now that Sora was upright, Pluto looked up at him and wagged his tail happily.

"Oh, boy… Do you know where we are?"

Huh? How did I…? As Sora wondered, Pluto ran on ahead.

Sora followed him into a district paved with brick—Traverse Town. And before him stood a mysterious figure with large black ears.

"Sora, this was the day that your journey began. I know, because I was here, too. It's time for the truth."

I don't have a clue what he's talking about. Or what this strange town is supposed to be. What's going on here? "Where am I? How'd I get here? And who are you?" Sora started peppering him with all the questions in his head.

"The name's Mickey. I've come here from another world," the guy—Mickey, apparently—explained. It wasn't much of an explanation, though.

"Seriously?" Sora asked.

"Ya see, somebody left me and my friends a mysterious message— 'Their hurting will be mended when you return to end it.' And you're the only one with the power to solve the mystery."

"Me? Why me?" Sora inclined his head quizzically as a large key—a Keyblade—immediately appeared in his hand in a flash of light. "Whoa!" he yelped.

This should have been his first time seeing it, and yet it felt right in his hand, as if he had always owned it. *It's like I've missed having it.*

"Good. You lost your memory, but not your powers," Mickey said with a bit of relief. "Will you help me, Sora? I need to know the truth."

Something stirred in his chest at Mickey's request.

"Gosh, but this is so weird. I don't even know you… Err, do I? Something about you does seem vaguely… Nah. So this truth you're after, does it have to do with me?"

Mickey smiled gently. Sora always had been an open book. "Honestly, I'm not sure. But whatever it is, I get the sense it's something you need to know."

"Hmm, fair enough…" *I guess I have a lot to do.* "All right, Mickey. Lead the way." *It's like there's a storm brewing in my chest…I think going with him will help with that, too.*

"Thanks, Sora! Now, just hold out that Keyblade of yours."

Sora did exactly that, while Mickey summoned his own Keyblade and lifted it to the sky. Light shot from the two Keyblades, opening a door, and the two stepped through to the other side.

They emerged into a spacious room built from something that looked like white marble.

The place seemed so cold and lifeless—the truth was here? Sora looked around, but there was no sign of Mickey. Maybe he had gone on ahead?

Seeing no other option, Sora started walking when a man appeared out of nowhere in front of him. He was covered head to toe by a hooded black coat.

"Huh?! Who are you?" Sora instinctively brought up his Keyblade. He couldn't even see the man's expression, let alone his face. And yet…was there something familiar about him?

"Me? I'm nobody," the hooded figure said quietly. "In this place, to find is to lose and to lose is to find. That's the way of things in Castle Oblivion."

"Castle Oblivion?" Sora repeated.

The man in black nodded and continued. "Yes… Here you will meet people you know. People you miss." He handed Sora a card. On it there was a picture of islands in a blue sea— *Hey, wait a sec…*

"Use that card and press on. You will find the truth that sleeps." With that, the man in the black coat vanished.

What did he mean, "use that card and press on"? Sora surveyed the room again, but the only way to go was through a door at the top of a nearby staircase.

Sora held the card out to the door, and it opened with a flash.

Beyond it was another white chamber much like this one, but it was littered with strange, unfamiliar blocks. What where they? As Sora puzzled over the question, the guy in black appeared again.

"That card you used will cause you to see people—illusions—who come from Jiminy's journal—the very same data you fixed."

"I fixed what? Who's Jiminy?" Sora didn't know what he was getting at. Mickey hadn't been making much sense, either, but this was even worse.

"Oh, my mistake. Did someone press the reset button on your memory? Just the same, you'll remember the folks you meet here."

"That makes zero sense. So I'm going to meet these...illusions, and then..."

There must be something I have to do.

But the man in black only had one thing to say, and it wasn't what Sora expected. "Do whatever you want."

"Huh?" Sora replied.

"There's no script you have to follow. The journal's the closest thing you've got, but that doesn't mean you'll see the things it says. And, you know, who really cares? Everything that happens here—everyone you meet—is an illusion."

How is that possible? Nothing is real? So I can do...whatever?

"Anything you want. But remember: the things that you find depend on the actions you take."

And with that, the black-coated man faded from view again.

"Hey, come back! ...He's gone..."

When Sora walked around exploring the area, he spotted a girl.

Isn't that...? "Selphie! What are you doing in a place like this?" he called to the girl in the yellow dress. Unlike Mickey and the guy in the black coat, he knew Selphie very well. She was a childhood friend from the islands.

"Uh, hello? I practically *live* on this island."

"This...'island'? You mean 'castle.'"

"No, I mean 'island,' but we can make-believe it's a castle if you want," Selphie said, a little confused. So she believed they were home on one of the islands. The man in the black coat had mentioned that the card would show him "illusions," but Sora couldn't tell if Selphie was the one seeing illusions, or if she herself was the illusion.

"Sora, you are acting so weird today! And where have you been, anyway? Would you look at the island? We're up to our ears in blocks!"

I knew that. I've heard someone say that before—but where?

"This is totally ruining my day. Do me a favor and find out where the blocks came from."

"Okay!"

Sora accepted the task pleasantly, and Selphie smiled. "Thanks, and good luck. I expect a thorough investigation."

Sora nodded to her and walked off. During his work destroying blocks, he saw Wakka with his ever-present blitzball.

"Hey! Sora! Things are gettin' hairy here, ya? You okay, brudda?"

"Umm… It's…been an…interesting day?" Sora tilted his head. He'd had this conversation before, hadn't he?

"That's great. Hey, could you check up on Tidus for me? He went to investigate the blocks."

Tidus must have wandered off, too.

"Sure!" Sora answered cheerily here, and then went on his way.

"Thanks, brudda! He can't have gone too far, but you know him," Wakka called. As he walked away, the guy in black appeared before Sora again.

"Don't let your memories rule your actions. Not when there are other possibilities to be found—other stories waiting to unfold." With that, he left yet again.

What does he mean? Stories different from before… Am I not supposed to look for Tidus?

Suddenly noticing the mound of blocks up ahead, Sora ran over to it with his Keyblade and destroyed it.

Once he was finished, the man in the black coat showed up again. "You found me—I'm impressed."

Sora was getting more and more dubious.

This time, when the guy disappeared, he was replaced by strange creatures—Heartless.

"Huh? What's going on?"

Sora managed to take down all the Heartless and, on a hunch, he took care of the blocks on the other side.

Sure enough, he showed up—the guy in the black coat. "More impressive still. But…let's see if you really have what it takes to keep up."

More Heartless arrived to take his place, and Sora poured all he had into beating them. Then—for the umpteenth time—the guy in black returned.

"Well, you did it again, Sora."

…Except this time, his voice was different.

"Wait…Riku? What are you doing here?"

Riku laughed a little beneath his hood at Sora's stunned reaction. "I've got something you need to see."

"Oh yeah?" Sora asked curiously.

"A hidden truth that isn't part of your memories," Riku replied. "I want you to see it. And, I want you to feel it."

A hidden truth that isn't part of my memories? I have no idea what that could be. Still…

"Well, okay. I know you wouldn't ask if it wasn't important." Sora gave him a sincere smile.

"Thanks, Sora. Close your eyes."

Sora quietly did just that. Light flickered across the back of his eyelids, and then he saw a big moon in the sky. He didn't recognize this place.

Riku was reaching out toward the moon. He closed his hand around it—but of course, he couldn't really pluck it out of the sky. He turned around, and behind him—was Kairi.

Sora's eyes blinked open.

"That's you and Kairi. I was on a journey to find you."

I remember now. But I don't quite understand how.

"Darkness had taken ahold of my heart, and Kairi had lost hers completely. But at the end of your journey, Sora, you would have saved us. Now, what did me and Kairi have in common? When you watched—what did you feel?" Riku asked softly.

"Umm..."

"It was 'hurt.' We had both lost ourselves, and we were hurting. So what would you have done?"

What kind of question was that? There was only one answer.

"Help you, of course! I would have figured out how to take the hurt away."

Sora couldn't see beneath Riku's hood, but he could tell his friend was wearing a warm little smile.

"I thought you'd say that. And you're right, you would. You will."

"Hmm... So what's with the sneak preview?" Sora crossed his arms and thought.

Riku took a step closer. Sora peered into the hood curiously, but he couldn't quite see the look on Riku's face.

"I just wanted you to see that you always make the right choices. On the road ahead, more than one truth will come to light. You'll forget things, lose things that you care about, and it won't always make sense. It may hurt so bad you'll feel like you're about to lose yourself. But you won't. Not you. You're like a sponge. No matter how much pain they throw at you, you'll suck it up, squeeze it out, and leave things a little better. Just follow your heart, and you can change lives. You don't have to do anything special. Just do what you do."

It's always a little hard to follow what Riku's talking about...but I know what he's getting at. Everything will work out if I keep following my heart as I always have and never give in.

"All right."

"Take care, Sora."

Sora gave a firm nod, and Riku vanished.

Suddenly, the world shimmered and blurred.

Next thing he knew, Sora was back in that big, pure white hall, and this time, the stranger in the black coat—the one who wasn't Riku—appeared as if he'd been waiting for Sora.

"Well? Did you have fun hanging with the ghosts?"

"Hey, don't say 'ghosts'! Sure, something was a little off, but they're still my friends." Sora bristled a little.

The figure in black seemed disappointed. "You don't say? What were their names again?"

"Pfft, that's easy. There was— What…? No, no, I know them! Why can't I remember?"

That's right, he couldn't remember. *I have no idea who I just met, or what I did.*

"Like I said, everything in this castle is an illusion. Your actions may lead to true endings or paradoxes, and each outcome will stay with you in the form of a card. But once the illusions vanish, you'll forget all about your little reunion as if it never happened."

"What?" *That's horrible. If this guy's the reason I'm forgetting, I won't let him get away with it.*

"Hey, no big deal. The fact that you can't remember them just means they weren't important to begin with."

"That's a lie! Of course my friends are important to me! Okay, so maybe I forgot who they are…and what happened…but it'll come back to me. Just watch!"

"Hmm. If you say so." The stranger snorted derisively and pulled out a set of cards. This time there were five of them.

"More cards?"

Sora looked at the cards. The first one depicted a nighttime townscape—he had a hunch he had seen it before somewhere. The second had a hedge maze in a garden. No clue about that one. On card number three was an arena where people could test their strength—no dice there, either. The fourth card depicted a palace in the desert. It didn't ring any bells. And on the fifth and final card, a castle loomed ominously. His heart sped up just looking at the pictures on the cards.

"All of these were created from data in the journal. And all of them will show you more illusions. But from now on, they won't be your friends. You're fresh off the island, which makes them total strangers. Here's a fun little thought: The folks you're about to meet? You can use and abuse them all you like."

"Huh?" *You can't do that...not to anyone.*

But the man in black wasn't done yet.

"What do you care? They're all strangers, and illusions at that. Just empty bits of data. They can't tell what's real. They'll look at this castle and see the world they call home. Anyway, the truth would be wasted on them. They're only there until they're not. See where I'm going with this? You can break the little hearts they don't have, and forget right away. No hurt feelings, no baggage. You don't have a heart. It's one-hundred-percent guilt-free."

"No, it's not." Sora refuted the idea flat-out.

"Oh?" asked the man in black.

"I could never be mean to somebody I just met," Sora replied firmly. "If I hurt them, I'd regret it. And...even if I didn't remember what I did, the regret would stay with me. That's what you mean by hurt feelings, right? Why would I want to carry around that kind of hurt?"

The stranger seemed to be smiling beneath his hood. "And with that, you've arrived at the first question," he murmured, fading away again.

"Huh?" *I have no idea what it is he's after. But...*

Sora looked at the five cards left in his hands. He was a bit nervous about using them to meet people he didn't know—but it also sounded fun.

Sora took the first card—the one of the town at night—and approached the door.

On the other side, in Traverse Town, Sora found some triplets safe and sound.

And yet...

The moment he returned, he could no longer recall who he had encountered a little while ago, or what he had done. His memory was a complete blank.

"Why do I feel so funny?" Sora pressed down on his chest in the hall. Something hurt inside. "I know...I miss them."

His chest—his heart—ached with loneliness. But if he was forgetting all about everyone he met, then he shouldn't miss anyone. That meant that at least some memories lingered. Or maybe it was that even if the memories were gone, a sliver of those feelings remained.

Given the right opportunity, he suspected it could all come back to him. For some reason, Sora felt like he had gained courage.

"Okay, let's do this!"

He held up the second card—with Wonderland, the labyrinthine garden on it—and offered it to the door.

In Wonderland, too, Sora encountered various people, answered several questions, and even had the queen put him on trial.

And when he finally returned, the guy in the black coat showed himself.

"So, how was your time with—I'm sorry, who was it again?"

"You know full well I can't remember," Sora answered somewhat nonchalantly. *It's fine if I forget. It'll come back to me again.*

"Heh. You seem pretty calm," said the man in black, and not exactly kindly. "Guess you decided they weren't worth stressing over. Out of sight, out of mind, right?"

"Wrong. I forgot them, like you said, but I can still feel them. I feel a lot of things. Frustrated... Lonely... You said there would be no hurt feelings. But I am hurting."

Sora could sense that the man was watching him intently beneath his hood.

"But…that's a good thing, right? Each time the memories slip away, they leave a hole. They leave hurt. But that hurt is the key to getting the memories back."

"…Right on schedule," said the stranger, to no one in particular. With that, he disappeared again.

Then, Sora held up the third card—the one depicting the arena, Olympus Coliseum.

There, Sora fought several battles, and met some friends. All of them were strong, he thought.

Upon returning to the hall, though, all of it was gone.

The loneliness, that awful loneliness, was being carved deeper and deeper into his heart.

The guy in the black coat greeted him once more. "The sadness of knowing you forgot someone who matters—that'll gnaw at you forever. And you believe carrying around that kind of hurt will bring back the memories you lost? Really, Sora?"

"That's the theory." Sora nodded resolutely.

The man in the coat laughed out loud.

"What's so funny?"

"I just can't believe you fell for it so easily."

"Fell for what?" Sora asked, somewhat angrily.

"I told you when you arrived," he quietly explained. "In this place, to find is to lose and to lose is to find. Well, you've lost your memories and found hurt in return. And by deciding that hurt was the key to remembering, you gave up all hope of ever being free from it!"

Hurt…isn't something you can just throw away. Of course it isn't. If Sora lost his loneliness, the memories really would be gone forever.

"Don't you see? The hurt owns you now, Sora. It's a wound that will never mend. That hole in your heart will grow bigger and bigger until darkness finally claims it!"

Do sadness, loneliness, and all those other painful emotions really lead to darkness? "So this was all some trick to drag me into the darkness?"

"Afraid so. And all it took was a handful of illusions. Your heart was just way too easy to break."

"Yeah, we'll see who breaks first!"

Sora had so many questions, but the man faded away before Sora could ask them.

His anxiety grew worse. Was this hurt actually a dark emotion? Either way, he had to keep pressing on to find out.

Sora held out the fourth card—Agrabah, the desert palace—to the door.

In Agrabah, Sora found a parrot hiding between some blocks.

When he came back, he forgot it all over again.

"It's not too late to run."

"What?"

As always, the guy in the black coat had arrived with his cryptic comments.

"You can still be free of the hurt. Just tell yourself you forgot them because they don't really matter. You'll have no one to miss. No cause for loneliness. No hurt to keep eating away at your heart."

Sora clenched his fist and held it tightly in front of his chest. *This hurt in my chest—if it goes away, then I won't be sad anymore...?*

"It's your call, Sora. Cling to the memories you've lost and the hurt they bring until it drags you into the darkness. Or...you could just let it all go. Be free. Be happy! Think it over." After he finished his piece, he was gone.

"Wait!" Sora wanted to go after him, but he was always too slow.

He didn't know what to do. There was only one card left. If he used it, he would meet someone else, forget them, and then experience another loss. That loss would hurt his heart. And the pain from those wounds would eventually overwhelm him, and he would succumb to the darkness.

Was his only salvation to let the pain go?

...ora? Sora! Can you hear me?

Sora had almost worried himself into a mental dead end when he heard Mickey's voice.
"M...Mickey? Is that you? Where are you?"

Sorry, I'm still trying to get to your position. Sending my voice is all I can manage for now.

Sora decided to pour out all his feelings to him. "That's okay. Hey, Mickey? I've got a problem here. I keep forgetting people in this place. And this guy in black—he says if I dwell on what I've lost, the hurt will take over."

Hmm... I see. So, will you let go of the people you've forgotten?

As Mickey asked this, two people appeared faintly before Sora. They weren't in his memories, though. He couldn't remember them.

You may not remember them, but they think of you as a friend.

He heard a very distinctive voice over Mickey's.

Wak! We've been on a ton of adventures together!

The next voice was easygoing and comforting.

A-hyuck! And even if you don't know who we are, Sora, you'll always be extra special to us.

A sudden warmth spread across Sora's chest, hearing those two. "But... Wait, how does that work?"

*   *   *

Ask your heart. What are you feeling right now?

"I feel... Well, I can't remember who they are. I don't think we've ever met. But I feel like...we belong together."

They seemed so, so familiar. Sora could feel courage and strength welling up within him.

Memories can disappear, but feelings don't—not even when your data was reset. Somewhere inside your heart, the adventures you shared with them in the datascape live on. And ya know what? So do all the folks those cards showed you.

Sora thought it over. *This pain in my heart is the same as that warmth I felt just now...?* As he mulled it over, the two vanished.

Uh-oh! Looks like I've used up a little too much of my power. I'll be there soon, Sora—I promise. Just hang on!

"Mickey?!" Sora called out, but there was no response. He was alone again—and very lonely. Was this feeling another kind of hurt? Would this hurt drag him into the darkness...?

He still had one card remaining. The creepy, towering castle—Hollow Bastion.

There was nowhere to go but forward.

In Hollow Bastion he fought two enemies and won, and the moment he came back, it was all gone. The man in black met Sora as if he had been lying in wait for him.

"You've used the last of the cards. I'd ask if you enjoyed the trip, but we both know you've forgotten. Bet you feel pretty empty."

"Anything but. I don't remember who I met, but I remember meeting them. And now that I've forgotten... I miss them." Sora placed a hand lightly on his chest. He lowered his gaze slightly. *Why can't I remember?*

"And so you hurt. Well, let's hope you didn't forget my warning. That hurt will drag you into the darkness. You have to cut it loose."

"…No. The hurt is what reminds me I've forgotten. It's proof there's something there, something…important. I won't run from it. It'll stay in my heart until the day I remember again."

I can't get rid of my pain. It's what lets me remember, deep down in my heart.

"You'll be lost in the darkness long before then."

"But if I put aside the hurt, I'll lose my only ties to people I cared about. No. My mind's made up—I want to carry this hurt with me. I can be free of it the day I remember, but until then, it's what holds together the pieces I left behind…and I accept it."

The stranger's shoulders were heaving up and down with fury. "You…accept it? Heh! Don't make me laugh! It's time you learned what real hurt feels like!"

The world was engulfed in a white light…

Sora found himself in a new, unknown world. There was nothing there but a cold, white floor hovering in the gloom. It brought a chill to his skin.

The man in the black coat was right in front of him with a Keyblade in each hand. In the span of an instant, he closed the gap between them and attacked Sora with both of them.

He landed a solid blow that knocked Sora away. For a moment, Sora felt pain—but not only physical pain. It was affecting his heart, too. What was this…?

With a shout, the man created columns of light around him to hit Sora again.

Maybe…the pain I felt then was the hurt of someone's heart? I feel it even more clearly than the pain in my body. It's hard to endure, but… something about it is almost comfortingly familiar, too.

It's a special hurt, born from the same thing as my lost memories.
I want to run away from it. But I won't.
Sora gripped his Keyblade tightly. "Haaah!"

Gathering his strength, Sora poured all his emotions into the attack. He landed hits, knocked his opponent back, and fired off spells.

But the black-clad man just got up again, floated into the air, and unleashed an incessant barrage of white light.

Sora evaded every one of the glowing orbs until he could get close again, and then he swung his Keyblade upward.

"—Nnh!" At last, the man in black fell to his knees. "Come on, Sora—do it! Finish me off," he gasped. Sora destroyed the man's Keyblades, then extended a hand to him.

"What are you...?" He rejected Sora's help and stood on his own. "Ah! Hmm. I guess you've seen through the last illusion: me. I'm data, just like the rest. Not even worth the effort, right? No point in destroying what never really existed. Heh."

However, Sora shrugged awkwardly with a little smile.

"For an illusion, you pack a punch!" *And the pain of those attacks showed me something...* "You weren't kidding about showing me some real hurt."

The man had nothing to say in reply to Sora's grin.

Maybe that shouldn't have come as a surprise. Sora continued speaking, more serious this time. "But the hurt I just felt is more than bumps and bruises... While we were fighting, I could feel the hurt in you."

Sora recalled what he had felt in the middle of their battle. It was a different sort of pain. He didn't know what made it special, but it was special all the same. That hurt had linked them.

"Sharp, intense pain...but familiar, somehow—almost like it was my own. It felt like we'd connected—like we shared the same hurt. If it brings me closer to people like that, then a little hurt can't be all that bad." Sora smiled at him again.

"'Can't be all that bad?' Heh. I give up. Here." The man in the black coat tossed a card to Sora. On it was an oddly shaped building Sora had never seen before. "You pass, Sora. You understand hurt. Now, use this to find the truth."

"What do you mean, 'pass'?" Sora inclined his head, looking at the card.

"My role was to see if you were ready to take ownership of the hurt inside you. And now that role is done. Nothing left for me to do but…go away."

"Go home?" Sora didn't know what he meant by go "away." Even if he was an illusion, going away sounded kinda…awful.

"I don't know if I have one, but…there's a place I'd like to be." For the first time, the man's tone softened.

"Where?" Sora asked.

Instead of answering, the man in the black coat approached—and merged with him.

"Huh?"

Sora was shocked as the man disappeared into him. But at that moment, when they became one, he felt a wave of nostalgia. It was most likely *his* memory—the recollection of the stranger in black.

He saw a place he had wanted to call home—a place he *had* once called home. The home he'd lost. A town at twilight; his first and last…

…summer vacation.

He heard the voice of the youth who had worn the black coat. In the back of his mind, he saw the boy smiling—Roxas.

"Rest easy… Your hurt can be mine now," Sora whispered, then gazed at the final card. *Time to get going.*

"Sora!" someone called.

Sora looked up, and running toward him was…

"Mickey!"

"I finally caught up to ya! Sorry I'm late. I didn't mean for you to do all the work."

"Don't even worry about it. Here, check this out!" Sora showed the last card to Mickey. "This card is supposed to lead to the truth."

"Hmm… Then maybe we'll finally find out where that mysterious message came from."

"Let's find out—together!"

Sora held the card up to the door, and the light it released washed over both him and Mickey.

Standing before them was a young girl with golden hair. Behind her was a large, flower-shaped capsule.

"Who are you?"

Sora was confused—she was so familiar. It was the same as when he met Mickey. There was no way they had met, and yet he felt as if he had fond memories of her.

"Nice to meet you. My name is Naminé. You don't know me, but I know you."

"Um…I don't really follow," Sora replied, perplexed.

"I'll explain," said Mickey. "At one point, you lost all of your memories, Sora. Naminé here is the person who saved you."

"Wow, then I owe you a lot!" Sora said with a smile.

Naminé shook her head in a slightly melancholy manner. "No, you really don't. It's true I put your scattered memories back together, but I'm also the one who took them apart in the first place. Not only that, the bugs that appeared in Jiminy's journal—those were my fault, too."

She lowered her gaze.

"What do you mean?"

Instead of answering Mickey's question, Naminé extended her right hand into the air, and a glowing orb rose from her palm. "It all began with these memories that were sleeping way down deep in Sora's heart."

"These are my memories?" Sora asked, looking at the fragment of memory Naminé had projected. Even after she lowered her hand, the twinkling fragment hovered in place. It was bright, almost too bright. So bright that touching it might even sting.

"No. Not yours. These belong to people connected to you."

"What? Isn't it weird for somebody else's memories to be inside me?"

Shouldn't I only have the memories of things I experienced myself?

"Right, it's not usually possible. When I first found them while repairing your memory, I thought I'd made a mistake. But all the evidence I found proved they belong in your heart, where they've been sleeping a long…long time. One day, Sora will have to call them to the surface. They're important memories…but very dangerous ones."

Sora didn't really understand what Naminé was saying.

"Dangerous how?" Mickey asked, while Sora was trying to make heads or tails of it.

"These memories are too painful. Handled the wrong way, they could damage Sora's heart—even break it. I needed you to find a way to face that kind of hurt. That's why I left the message."

Their hurting will be mended when you return to end it.

That was the message in the journal.

"That was you?"

This time, Naminé nodded at Mickey. "When I unraveled Sora's and the others' memories, you remember it also erased the words from Jiminy's journal? Well, that shows how deeply the journal and Sora are connected. When I took Sora's memories apart, they stayed in his heart and in the journal even after the text was gone. That's why you were able to render them as data."

Sora still had no clue what Naminé was saying as he watched Mickey listen to her story with some concern.

"But the data was a mess because of all the bugs. Jiminy never wrote any of that stuff down," Mickey said.

"No…that was me. When I added these memories to the journal, I added 'hurt.' I thought that maybe if you fought the bugs that sprung from these memories, you might learn to face the hurt in the memories themselves." Naminé lowered her gaze again. This seemed to be difficult for her.

"Gosh, you sure went through a lot of trouble."

"I'm sorry." Naminé bowed her head. "I wish I could have told you all this in person. But the real me is gone now."

The "real me"…? So where's the real Naminé? Um, and if this is a world inside some data, then…huh? Then where—who is the real me? I'm this guy Sora, and Sora is me, but then this is a world made from memories, so…?

Sora let out a long sigh, then smiled. "Um…guys? This is all way over my head… Am I dumb?"

Naminé laughed. "Of course not. After all, you did it. You learned how to face the hurt."

"I did?"

Sora cocked his head to one side. While it was true that he hadn't decided to cast aside his hurt during the fight with the boy in the black coat, he still didn't know how to face it down. All he had done was decide to hold on to it.

"Some people think pain is something you can just wipe away—and sometimes, maybe, you can. But not all pain can be erased. The only way to deal with it is to accept it head-on."

Maybe they're the same thing—accepting it head-on and choosing not to throw it away.

Naminé continued. "And if the hurt is too great for you to bear it alone—well, then you turn to a friend close to your heart."

"Because the hurt will bring us closer together and make us stronger," Sora said quietly, taking in what she was saying. He looked up at the light hovering before him.

"Right, let's give it a try!" he declared.

Naminé gave Sora a confused look.

"With the memories you found. I'm ready to accept them, no matter how painful they are."

"Sora…"

Naminé gave him a brief nod. Before Sora could reach out his hand, Mickey ran up to him. "Wait! I'll join you."

"Okay!" Sora turned toward Mickey and nodded. He might not be able to handle them on his own, but with the two of them, it was sure to work.

"Thank you." Naminé also looked up at the memory fragment. "Touch this, and the memories locked inside will flow into your hearts."

Sora and Mickey linked hands, and then reached out toward the light. The radiance from the memories was almost too strong, and pain coursed into them the moment they touched it. It hurt so much, it was hard to breathe. Their chests were getting tighter and tighter.

"Stay strong, Sora!"

At Mickey's encouragement, Sora squeezed his eyes shut and clenched his teeth. Eventually, behind his eyelids a hazy image of two people appeared through the light. Their backs were turned to him.

"Who…?"

Both were wearing black coats. One was a guy who looked just like the one Sora had fought earlier. The other was a redhead he didn't know. Roxas and Axel.

"Ah!" Mickey cried in astonishment.

"These are hidden truths that Sora has been keeping locked away deep inside him. Remember, these memories aren't his," Naminé said quietly.

The duo disappeared, to be replaced by another pair. One was Naminé, the other a black-haired girl with a black coat like the first two. She looked a lot like Naminé. Right—her name was Xion.

He didn't think he knew those four, but Sora felt a painfully wistful yearning, and a grief that threatened to crush his chest.

Is this hurt…?

"These people are waiting for Sora—the only one who can put an end to their hurt. DiZ told me he did something inside you during the year you were asleep. I asked him what, and all he would say was that he was 'clearing his conscience.' Sora must be the key to saving the people you saw—"

The other Naminé and the black-haired girl vanished from the white light, and this time three more strangers surfaced: a young man, a woman, and the third…was a boy who looked a lot like the first young man. Terra, Aqua—and Ven.

"—and these ones, too."

"It can't be!" Mickey cried out again.

"Maybe you know how much they're hurting."

Sora opened his eyes and saw that Naminé was gazing at him quietly.

"These three were keys, too. connected to the truth behind the Keyblade. And they're still connected, Sora, somewhere way down deep inside of you."

"Funny. I feel as though…I've met them," Sora whispered. He didn't remember, though.

"Yes, two of them, you have met. As for the third…I never realized it, but…you and he share a very special connection."

I don't get it, but I can still feel the connection.

"Naminé. You said Sora has to call these memories to the surface. Is it time?" Mickey asked. It was possible that he, too, knew something about the trio.

"I can't say for sure. But I do know a day will come when they must rise from their sleep. And then the only one who can save them… will be Sora." Naminé smiled at him.

"The bond they all share—that's gonna be the key, right?" Mickey let go of Sora's hand and looked up at Naminé. "Don't worry, Naminé. I'll make sure I pass this on to Sora—you know, the one in the outside world!"

"Mm, please do."

Mickey nodded deeply to Naminé.

"Well—"

"Just a second." Sora interrupted Naminé's farewell.

She tilted her head to the side. "Huh?"

"Our promise… Your promise to the me I don't know. You kept it, right?" he asked.

Her gaze turned distant. "I may be gone, but my promises to him are forever. And anyway…I owe this much. For all the…all those people that I hurt." She shook her head sadly.

"So what happens to you? The one that's right here?"

"I'm really just data made to pass along a message. I shouldn't… exist right now in this journal at all. And now, the record of me will disappear. But when you pass my message on to the other Sora, just remember to tell him the things that you've seen…and that you've felt. If you do that, then we'll be at rest—her, and me too."

The other Sora, the other Naminé who was gone…and all the other people who'd made him who he was.

"Along with everybody connected to Sora… Naminé, you got it." Now, Sora knew the truth.

"Okay." Naminé smiled at him.

"Oh yeah! I almost forgot. I have a message for you, too." Sora gazed at Naminé.

Somehow, he knew he had to tell her this, no matter what.

"Thank you."

She was startled at first, but her expression soon turned to a smile.

And then, still smiling, Naminé silently vanished.

"And so ended our journey to connect 'those' memories with 'these.'"

I wanted to tell you right away...about memories from the past that sleep within you,
and about the pieces that will tie you to your future.

Sora, Riku, Kairi... The truth behind the Keyblade has found its way through so many people, and now I know that it rests in your hearts. Sora... You are who you are because of those people, but they're hurting, and you're the only one who can end their sadness. They need you.

It's possible that all your journeys so far have been preparing you for this great new task that's waiting for you. I should have known there were no coincidences—only links in a much larger chain of events.

And now the door to your next journey is ready to be opened.

——Yen Sid, I think we're finally close to figuring out where Ven's heart is.

——Is that so? Then that leaves only Terra.

——Right. And we've gotta save all three of them.

——Hmm... The question is: What does Xehanort intend to do next?

——Xehanort? But his two halves are gone. There was Ansem, who commanded the Heartless, and Xemnas, who commanded the Nobodies. Didn't Sora defeat them both?

——Correct, those two met their end. However, therein lies exactly our problem. Their destruction now guarantees the original Xehanort's reconstruction. Xehanort's heart, once seized by his Heartless half, is now free. And his body, which had become his Nobody, has been vanquished. Both halves will now be returned to the whole. In short...this means Master Xehanort will return.

——And you think...you think that maybe he's gonna try something?

——A man like Xehanort will have left many roads open.

——Well, it doesn't matter what he cooks up. Me and Sora, we'll be ready. And Riku, too!

——Yes, they are indeed strong. But...not true Keyblade Masters, like you. Tell me...would a single one of you suffice if what you faced was not a single one of him?

——What? What do you mean?"

——Mickey, please summon Sora hither? Riku as well.

——Of course, but...why?

——To show us the Mark of Mastery.